a

o

n

M

'A

pr

BE

OT

'Ell

of our planet and ... scheming adults – she'd

do Greta Thun... ndromes, leaps

across time and ... KIM ZARINS,

author of SOM... UTH

'In this inventive, mind-boggling tale, Agbabi introduces us to Elle – a determined, autistic, time-travelling crimefighter – whose voice will charm and astonish readers everywhere' STEVE TASANE, author of CHILD I

'Wonderful . . . *The Infinite* is a gripping, funny, futuristic story, brilliantly structured and humanely told in vivid language with a lively cast of characters that will charm, alarm and surprise readers of all ages' CAROLYNE LARRINGTON, author of WINTER IS COMING

'Fans of Hayley Long's *Sophie Someone* will love this imaginative time-travelling caper. A nail-biting adventure!' JULIA FORSTER, author of WHAT A WAY TO GO

THE INFINITE

PATIENCE AGBABI

First published in Great Britain in 2020 by Canongate Books Ltd,
14 High Street, Edinburgh EH1 1TE

canongate.co.uk

1

British Library Cataloguing-in-Publication Data
A catalogue record for this book is available on request from the British Library

ISBN 978 1 78689 965 1

Typeset in Horley Old Style MT by Palimpsest Book Production Ltd,
Falkirk, Stirlingshire

Printed and bound in Great Britain by Clays Ltd, Elcograf S.p.A.

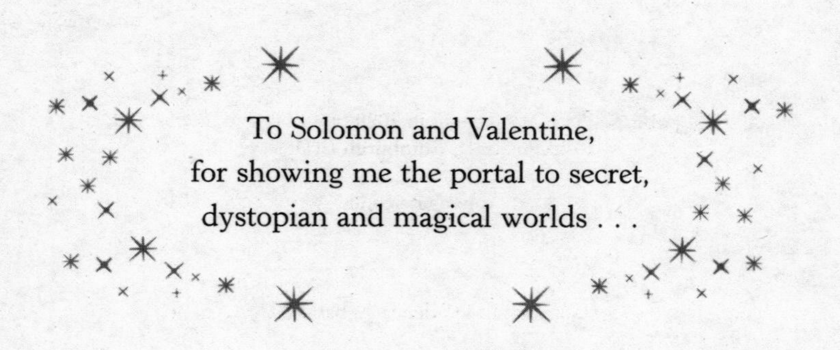

To Solomon and Valentine,
for showing me the portal to secret,
dystopian and magical worlds . . .

Some people say that we are fighting for our future,
but that is not true. We are not fighting for our future,
we are fighting for everyone's future.

– Greta Thunberg

Contents

Chapter 01:00

ELLE

Something bad just happened and I want to leap back in time to make it unhappen.

But you're not supposed to solo leap till you're 3-leap, which is 12 years old for Annuals.

I won't be 3-leap until the 29th of February. Three days' time.

I just ran out of double geography and now I'm in the corridor. I'm tongue-tied and my face is burning red with humiliation and I can still hear Mr Carter's old, creaky voice in my memory: 'Elle, where are you going?'

I check my watch: 15:01, Wednesday 26 February.

I close my eyes to block out the muffled shouts from the classroom, the yellow walls of the corridor, the smell of sweat and all the bad thoughts colliding in my head about the bad thing that happened AND getting into trouble for running out of a lesson.

I'm THINKING about leaping back in time so the bad thing won't happen. I don't MEAN to leap. That would be wrong.

When I have that thought, another one comes into my mind at the same time. Will athletics club still be on tonight? It's usually 5 o'clock on a Wednesday, but someone said it might be cancelled. I imagine doing running round the track to keep myself calm and it feels like it's actually happening. My body goes fizzy, charged up like a battery. Something very strange is happening to me. My body isn't any bigger but it's much stronger. I'm no longer Elle, I'm Elle to the power of 3! My head begins to spin so fast I stop thinking about running. I try to think about nothing at all but I've never felt so happy, like I could take on the whole world.

I clasp my hands tight.

Everything goes dark.

I hear a door open.

Classroom chatter pours out, like a tidal wave.

∞

I open my eyes. Things slowly come into focus, like my eyes are a camera. I'm sitting on the grass by the school track, next to the long-jump pit. My watch says 17:00. My mouth is a capital O. I just leapt 1 hour 59 minutes into the future!

I feel dizzy, like I've been in the spin dryer at the laundrette and my skin's still damp. When I try to move, I throw up all over the grass. But it doesn't make me sad; it makes me feel better. I look around me. No one's doing slow jog or high knees. No one's spinning in the discus circle. Athletics really is off tonight. So, nobody saw me appear out of thin air; nobody saw me leap from the corridor.

Only you and I know what just happened.

I'm tongue-tied with everyone. Except you. It's easier talking to you because I don't know what you look like or if your eyes are rolling clockwise or anticlockwise because I said something odd or rude like 'How many days have you suffered from acne?'

I'm autistic, so sometimes I'm very direct or say the wrong thing at the wrong time. But I LOVE words, the sound and shape of them and how they feel on my tongue. And I love sprinting and long jump because it's the closest you get to flying. And when I TALK about sprinting and long jump, it's like the words come to life and I'm pounding down the runway, launching myself into the air. It's the best thing ever.

I like it here beside the track. If I was a millionaire, I'd build my house right here.

How fast can you run the 100 metres? My PB's 13.12 seconds, which gives me an 89.59% age grade. That means I'm almost in the top 10% in the world for 11 year olds. I want to run in the Olympics and stand a good chance because I'm a Leapling with The Gift and the Olympics only happens in a leap year.

My favourite Olympics is Mexico City, 1968.

My favourite athlete of all time is Bob Beamon.

Bob Beamon made a world record in the long jump of 8.90 metres at the 1968 Olympics.

They had to send someone out of the stadium to buy an old-fashioned tape measure so they could measure the jump properly.

Mr Branch, my athletics coach, says it was the most political Olympics since 1936, when Jesse Owens got four gold medals and made Hitler leave the stadium. In 1968, Tommie Smith and John Carlos did the Black Power salute wearing black gloves on the medal podium and got suspended from the US team. Dick Fosbury raised his fist during his medal ceremony in solidarity with Black Power. Dick Fosbury was white. He invented a new way of doing the high jump called the Fosbury Flop.

But the best part of the 1968 Olympics was Bob Beamon's jump.

∞

It's 17:10 and Grandma will be home in 20 minutes, so I need to run home. There's still frost on the opposite pavement and cracked ice on the puddles, even though the sun came out today. I love weather like this. It doesn't happen very often in February. Usually it's grey, cloudy and damp. I wonder what the weather will be like in the future. If it gets warmer, we won't get frost any more and people will read about it in history books.

I suddenly realise how cold it is, that I leapt out of school without my coat and now school's closed. But you don't need a coat if you're running. You just run and run and run and feel warm inside and the air feels cool on your skin. I grab my bag and run across the school fields, the frost crunching under my feet, jump over the fence like in the steeplechase and start running up the tree-lined drive that leads to the Hill. You'd think after leaping I'd be tired but it's the opposite. I feel like I could run a marathon.

It's not a steep hill but it goes on for ages. It's next to the main road, and there isn't much traffic, so it really is like running a marathon in the Olympics when they get rid of the traffic so the runners don't get run over. But I don't run on the road, I run on the path. The council haven't cut the hedge so I have to be careful not to get cut on the thorns.

There's lots of houses on both sides of the road with their windows boarded up and piles of rubbish stinking in the gardens. You know people still live there because the bins are overflowing. Grandma says they're flats where they put criminals when they come out of prison and have no money. The bins smell horrible. The council never empty them. I breathe through my nose, even though Mr Branch says it's better to breathe through your mouth to get more oxygen. It's hard running uphill with a schoolbag full of books, my geography project which I didn't hand in, my yam and my PE kit.

When I reach the top of the hill, I'm in the zone. The zone is when you get into your running rhythm and forget where you are. I like being in the zone. It feels safe, like being under the table when I want to calm down. But there's a car horn hooting, hooting, hooting. I turn my face to see a bright red car and a woman with long ginger hair. It's Mrs C Eckler, my favourite teacher. She stops, winds down the window and says something about school and athletics and giving me a lift but I'm panicking that I won't be home before Grandma, who will find out athletics wasn't on and wonder why I didn't get home earlier. Panic makes me hear her words in the wrong order and my heart starts thumping. Lots of cars are queuing behind her, hooting their horns. It's all too much. I accelerate away like Usain Bolt.

The path's level now. I run past the shops, the newsagent's, the Indian grocer's, the Polish deli that had its windows smashed in so there's cardboard in their place. Someone sprayed graffiti onto it in a foreign language I don't understand. We buy bread there sometimes because it's nicer than the bread in the supermarket and the same price. I start to relax now that I can't hear those cars hooting like an orchestra from hell.

I'm in the centre of town now. I run through the Pound Emporium, even though the floor's slippery and the flickering overhead lights always give me a headache, and out the other side to the car park, where they sometimes have a market selling bruised fruit. I go this way because there aren't as many people. I run past the big supermarkets we never go to because Grandma's leg pains her when she walks more than 200 metres, and on past the industrial estate.

This is the best part of town. Old, grey buildings used by businesses, and no people. It's the best place to run. The windows look like eyes with no sockets and sometimes big lorries go in making a rumbling noise like they've taken over from human beings.

We live in a flat on the other side of the industrial estate in a row of houses nicknamed 'The Mush-Rooms'. I think they're called that because the walls are so damp mushrooms grow out of them. Our landlord's Italian and he doesn't charge the same rent as the English ones. Most of the people who live there are Nigerian or Polish, except Mrs Leggett, who acts like she owns the place. The houses are terraced, so I can hear what people are saying in the next flat, though Grandma says that's not possible with old houses. But I can.

I'm starting to get tired but have a second wind when The

Mush-Rooms come into view. I do a sprint finish and only stop running when I reach our front door, number 36.

∞

When she comes through the flat door, even though she's out of breath from walking up the stairs, Grandma sings 'Elle Bíbi-Imbelé!' and looks at me with her what-big-eyes. Most people just call me Elle. My full name is Elle Bíbi-Imbelé Ifíè. I write it with accents so people say it properly but they still get it wrong. Ifíè means time in Izon, which is a Nigerian language. Bíbi-Imbelé means mouth-sweet, as in sweet-talking. I like having time as one of my names and I like sweet-talking, except when I'm tongue-tied, and I love Elle because it's a palindrome like Hannah. It reads the same backwards and forwards. Before she died, Mum called me Elle after the fashion magazine.

Grandma says Mum died before I was born. But that doesn't make sense, does it? Grandma says Mum was in a coma after the car crash, so it was like she was dead. Maybe that's what she means. After Mum died, my dad went back to Nigeria and married someone else. I don't miss my mum or dad because I don't remember them. Grandma's like a mum to me. She's very short for a grown-up.

I was the same size as Grandma two years ago. People say 'Elle, you're tall for your age' but they don't know my TRUE age. I'm not 11 going on 50 like Mr Branch says. I'm two going on three. I bet you've guessed why. I'm a bissextile, a Leaper, or Leapling. I only celebrate my birthday every four years.

This Saturday I'll be 3-leap. And I'm going on a school trip to 2048! We'll be staying at the Time Squad Centre. Only four pupils from my class were chosen. They sent secret letters to our parents six weeks ago and I had to read mine out to Grandma because she can't read or write but still puts on her glasses like she can. I was so excited and scared, I almost went tongue-tied. My favourite line from the letter was: 'Elle has been chosen for this trip because she scored the highest for Effort in Past, Present and Future for the whole of Seventh Year.'

Leaplings are just like Annuals, but a tiny percentage of us have The Gift. I had to swear the Oath of Secrecy on my 2-leap birthday after Grandma discovered what made my body fizz. She swore the Oath, too. The room was round and dark, with no windows, and whichever way I looked there were people holding hands with each other. I didn't know which way to face. The walls smelled of the woods after it's rained. One voice said my Gift was extraordinary. I love that extra ordinary means very, VERY ordinary but extraordinary means the opposite. Big Ben has worked out The Gift is super rare. Only 0.6% recurring of Leaplings have it. If you let him, Big Ben would say 0.6666666 6666666666666666666666666666 and keep on going to infinity.

Big Ben's in the same class as me at school. He's autistic too. He has short, scruffy hair that's blond and brown at the same time, though he's never had it streaked, a round face and extremely long legs. He corrects Mrs Grayling in double maths on a Tuesday afternoon and she gets cross. His real name is Benedykt Novak, which is Polish. Grandma likes his name because it means blessed and her own name is Blessing Ifîè. He's called Big Ben because of his height and obsession with timing things.

Big Ben has a stopwatch that times things down to two decimal points. He times me doing the 100 metres even when I don't want him to. He can't help it. He times EVERYTHING. And throws chairs when he goes from 0 to 10 on the anger scale. Big Ben's already been excluded from two schools. At his first school, he overturned his desk and books went everywhere. He'd only just started Second Year but was very strong. He went to the same primary school as me after that. In Sixth Year, he threw a chair because the teacher told him off for talking when he wasn't. It landed on the teacher's desk and snapped like firewood. Everyone cheered except the teacher and me. I missed him when he left.

Intercalary International's his last chance. After that, it's the Pupil Referral Unit. That's a school for children who get excluded and they can't find another school to take them on. I worry Big Ben will end up there one day. He never remembers to do time-out. When I do time-out, I do running round the playground or the athletics track. He doesn't throw chairs at people now, though, just at tables or chairs with no one sitting in them. Zero occupancy.

Big Ben's favourite car is a Lamborghini Asterion, which goes from 0 to 60 in three seconds, but his ambition is to time its acceleration down to a nanosecond. That's a billionth of a second. His uncle's a second-hand-car dealer. Last year he told Big Ben he'd teach him to drive when he was tall enough. He didn't expect that Ben would grow 6 inches that year. Now Big Ben can drive better than his uncle, even though he's exactly the same age as me and it's illegal to drive a car until you're 17.

Everyone thinks he's my boyfriend but he's not. I hang out with him because he's clever and kind and times me when I'm running. He says I'm the best sprinter in athletics club because I'm faster than boys the same age. Once I was crying at school because Pete LMS kept repeating everything I said in a silly voice so the teacher gave him detention. Big Ben gave me one of his socks straight off his foot. It was dark grey, at least a size 10 and smelled of cheese. I hid it in my bag because people might make more fun of me but it made me feel much happier. Big Ben doesn't care what people think. He'd never give me perfume or flowers just because I'm a girl. He says 'Am I your boyfriend?' 100 times a day.

∞

Grandma's plaiting my hair before bed. I love it when she plaits my hair, even when she cornrows it so tight that I can't close my eyes in bed for the first night. She says it must last a long time so the tighter the better, but it pulls my skin so I look like I've had a facelift. It takes days for my face to feel normal!

Tonight, she's doing single plaits I can comb out in the morning. I sit on the floor and she sits on the sofa behind me, combs my hair with the afro comb, then the fine-tooth comb to divide it into sections. She massages pomade into my scalp, which smells like tar but in a good way. Some of the other pomades used to make me sick so we only buy this one. When I start shuffling on my bottom, shifting from one side to the other because I find it hard to sit still on the prickly carpet, Grandma sucks her teeth.

'Elle Bíbi-Imbelé! You are too antsy-pantsy. Sit, not run-o!'

Grandma likes singing my name. Tonight, she's happy. I know she's happy because she's singing whilst plaiting my hair AND she doesn't have to work hard to pull it tight when she's tired after a day of cleaning because it only has to last till the morning. I'm happy too because it won't feel like a facelift and I'll be able to close my eyes in bed.

But when I get into bed and close my eyes I don't sleep, I worry.

I worry Mrs C Eckler was so offended I ran away from her she'll stop being nice to me in school and won't be my favourite teacher any more.

I worry someone will find out about the illegal leap and arrest me and send me to a Young Offenders Unit, which is prison for teens, though I'm not 3-leap yet.

But most of all I worry about the bad thing that happened at school.

I open my eyes wide to make the bad thoughts go away but it doesn't make any difference. My mind plays back today like a film on a loop. Each time I see it, it's exactly the same as the first time. Every sight, every sound, every smell. It's bad because, even though I now know it's going to happen, I don't know what it means.

Today I got a text from the future!

Chapter 02:00
THE PREDICTIVE

My school is called Intercalary International because it's a boarding school for Leaplings who have The Gift. It only has two classes with a four-year gap in between and goes up to Fourteenth Year. It looks like a country mansion and you have to go up a drive with lots of tall trees to get to it. There's no sign outside apart from 'Private' because it's top secret. Locals think an eccentric billionaire lives there. It's the only one in the world and some of the pupils come from places like India and Brazil.

I'm a day pupil because I live close by. Very occasionally, an Annual will attend as a day pupil if they're the right age and can't fit into another local school, like Pete LMS. His real name is Peter Wolf and he's a bully. He goes to athletics club, but Mr Branch never picks him for the team. He went to my primary school. In Second Year, he was addicted to the computer, wanted everyone to 'Like My Status' on Facebook = HIS status, not mine. I never go on Facebook because of trolls. I nicknamed him Pete LMS and the name stuck. EVERYONE calls him Pete

LMS. He's still addicted to social media. I never call him Pete LMS to his face. I wouldn't want to get close to his face anyway. His breath smells of raw meat.

Yesterday we had double PPF before lunch. Leaplings don't do history, we do PPF, which stands for Past, Present and Future. We take PPF in Block T, away from the main school building and built in the shape of a capital 'T'. The further up the school you go, the more lessons you have in Block T. We don't mix with the Eleventh Years until after the first Leap trip. PPF's my favourite subject. I got a Level 4, which is exceptional for a Seventh Year.

Yesterday was important in the PPF curriculum. Our teacher, Mrs C Eckler, gave us final information about the Leap 2048 trip to the Time Squad Centre. The Time Squad is like the Crime Squad, but it solves crimes committed across YEARS rather than countries, like if you kill someone in 2020 and hide the body in 1960. It only has four members of staff and is also top secret.

In Seventh Year you go to the future because it doesn't matter if you get things wrong. You have to be more experienced before you leap to the past. You do that in Eleventh Year. If you accidentally change something in the past, you rupture the space–time continuum. It's a VERY BIG DEAL. But some people say you can't change the past because what happened, happened. I prefer the past: you know what's going to happen. I'd rather go back to 1968. The future is totally unpredictable.

We were given the timetable for the Leap 2048 trip last week, but Mrs C Eckler said it might change because of the weather.

In 2048 it rains so much due to global warming they've invented new words for it, like drazzle and catdogs. I was surprised they hadn't improved weather forecasts by then so people could plan things. I like plans. They help make things more predictable so I feel safe. When plans change, everything becomes unpredictable.

Then, Mrs C Eckler introduced us to the Meat Ration menu.

'Can anyone tell me why meat is rationed in the future? Yes, Elle.'

'Meat is rationed in the future because too many people want to eat it for dinner and they ran out of land to breed enough animals to be made into meat.'

After that, lots of the meat became GM, which means genetically modified. I learnt that in science. Even now, scientists can change genes to make animals grow faster or lose their horns. In the future, people became scared it would make THEM grow faster or, worse still, GROW horns, so some stopped eating meat. But millions still wanted to eat meat that wasn't GM. So it had to be rationed.

The Time Squad have a no meat policy to be eco-friendly. On the lunch menu, there were things like minute steaks made of beans. Mrs C Eckler asked me to read the menu out loud because I have a clear voice. I pronounced minute steaks miNUTE by mistake. Mrs C Eckler corrected me and said it was MInute, as in $\frac{1}{60}$ of an hour. I felt humiliated but Mrs C Eckler said she'd made the same mistake herself which made me feel so much better.

Yesterday, Mrs C Eckler gave us a quiz about 2048 to

see if we'd been listening in class. It had questions about eco-robots who collect rubbish. I liked it because it was multiple choice, which means they give you some silly answers, some not-so-silly, and the correct one, and you have to choose. I like reading the silly answers best because they're like jokes. The best ones were:

Question 2: Why must we keep the Time Squad trip a secret?
Answer B said: To stop the wristwatch becoming extinct.
The correct answer was C: Because we all swore the Oath of Secrecy to protect The Gift and everything connected with it.

Question 6: Why is the population smaller than in 2020?
Answer E said: Everyone went to live on the moon!
The correct answer was A: The global one-child-per-family policy.

There was one I had to guess.

Question 7: What was significant about the year 2000?
I put A: The Time Squad was formed.

But I thought it might have been C: There was an upsurge of eco-crimes.

I couldn't remember if the upsurge BEGAN in 2000 or just after.

After that, she showed a video about the Time Squad Centre.

First '2020' came onto the screen followed by a picture of the globe with green for land and blue for water. Then '2048', and there was more blue on the globe. The camera zoomed into the green really quickly, so it was like the view from a plane. Rain seemed to be dripping down the camera lens.

The camera zoomed in again on an aerial view of a glass building surrounded by lots of fields and trees green as a tropical rainforest, a play park with everything made of wood and a group of yellow dome-shaped buildings that looked like upside-down baskets. It was still raining.

Big letters on the screen said 'FIGHT CRIME ACROSS TIME'. That's the Time Squad motto. A voice said, 'Welcome to Time Squad Centre, 2048,' and the camera zoomed in on an old white woman. Her face was like earth when it hasn't rained for months, her hair was a white electric shock and she had cat's eyes. She looked 200 years old. A caption said 'MILLENNIA, Centre Director' and she said, 'I run the Centre.' I smiled when she used the word 'run', imagining her sprinting down the track in the 100 metres, doing a dip finish.

Then the camera zoomed in on the grass and trees and showed a bald man chopping wood who looked about 40. Lots of letters were flying around like insects, which made me feel dizzy until they settled into words, a caption, which said 'LE TEMPS, Eco-landscaper' and Le Temps was a talking head. He said, 'I plan the land,' and I was surprised because I expected him to have a French accent but he just sounded posh. I know *le temps* means weather in French so maybe he was in charge of the weather as well. He wasn't doing a very good job!

Then the camera went into the building and zoomed in on a café sign, with green tendrilly writing on a white background that read 'The Beanstalk', then into a large white room with a brown floor with a giant beanstalk in the middle that went right up into the ceiling, and it focused on a fat woman who was older than Le Temps but younger than Millennia and looked Indian. She was kneading a big lump of white dough like it was a punchbag. Her long black hair had silver streaks and it was wound up into a knot on top of her head and she had her nose pierced with a sparkly blue stone. The caption said 'SEASON, Cook' and she became a talking head. She said, 'I make the food.'

Then the camera went along a corridor and up a spiral staircase to a door that said 'The Igloo' and went inside. The room was round, with large white bricks and a dome ceiling. Then a teenage boy appeared out of nowhere, disappeared, appeared again in another part of the room, and I recognised him because he came to our school last year at the beginning of Seventh Year. He looked exactly the same: a skinny black boy with hair like antennae and white clothes with graffiti on them. A caption came up saying 'MC^2, Energiser'. I assumed he charged us up like batteries. The camera zoomed in on his face and he blinked several times before he said, 'I move through time and space,' and Big Ben pumped his arm in the air. That was the end of the video.

Mrs C Eckler turned off the equipment and smiled.

'Any questions? Yes, Ben.'

'In 2048, are we 40 years old?'

'No, Ben. When we leap, we'll all stay the same age as now.

But you've raised a very important issue.' She cleared her throat, so I knew she was going to say something important. 'Very rarely, when people leap they meet their future self. Your FUTURE self would be 40.'

I raised my hand. 'Is it dangerous?'

'No, Elle. But you mustn't approach your future self. Let them approach you. They will know exactly what to do.'

I still wasn't sure Big Ben's future self would be less likely to go from 0 to 10 than him. I had lots more questions, like how MC^2 was going to charge us up like batteries, but they stayed in my head, which was resting on the desk straight after the video. I'd already started replaying it back in my mind, especially Season kneading a big lump of white dough. I knew we had breadmaking in the timetable and wondered if we were going to make WHITE bread. I hoped so because I only eat white food. If the food has a colour, or worse still lots of different colours on the same plate, the smell and flavour mixed with the SIGHT of it is too much and I get sensory overload and have to have time-out. I don't want to eat with my eyes closed.

I was still thinking that when I realised Mrs C Eckler was talking to me.

'Elle, be ready for me to collect you at 5:45 a.m. this Saturday. Text me if you're feeling delicate.'

I looked up at her. 'Why will I feel delicate?'

'Sometimes we have an Oops, remember. Things happen that we don't expect. If you're feeling a BIT delicate, you can still come on the trip. But we must plan for Oops.'

Oops is the bane of my life. Oops makes my heart beat fast

and hard like I just ran the 100 metres but instead of feeling happy I feel scared. If there was a person called Oops, they'd be my mortal enemy. Worse than Pete LMS. Mortal enemy means you fight to the death.

∞

After lunch was double geography. We've been doing projects on climate change and what we can do to stop it. We had to interview grown-ups about food, fossil fuels or plastic bags. I interviewed Grandma about food. I don't want the climate to change because I find it difficult when it goes from spring to summer and autumn to winter. The government make the clocks go forwards or backwards, it's either too dark or too light and messes with my sleep. It takes me weeks to recover. But the worst thing is when weather changes dramatically from one day to the next. I have to check the forecast a lot because the prediction can change every hour, especially when it's windy. The wind makes the weather move around like a poltergeist.

Projects mean working in pairs and I was with Big Ben. He wanted to do CO_2 emissions from cars. He plans to invent the first eco-friendly supercar. But I wanted to do the meat and dairy industry because I read online that the rainforest is being destroyed so they can grow cows to make into burgers. When the cows poo they mess up the gases in the air, so the air gets warmer and melts icebergs in the North Pole and sea levels rise.

Grandma told me when she was a girl she only ate meat once a year at Christmas, when they killed a goat and roasted it for the whole village. The rest of the time they ate fish from the river like tilapia. I was happy when she told me that because I like fish even more than meat. But when I read about us fishing too many fish until there will be none left I was sad.

I wanted to celebrate vegetables. I brought a yam into school as an example of a vegetable. Big Ben had to go with my idea because he has difficulty reading and talking in class unless it's maths or PPF. Anyway, he wasn't at school yesterday because of Anger Management so I had to present on my own.

I got to geography last because I always try to avoid the rush between lessons. As soon as I walked through the door I heard, 'Where's your Leaper boyfriend?' It was Pete LMS. He always says this when Big Ben isn't at school. Some of the class laughed, but Jake smiled at me and Maria said:

'Shut up! You're not funny.'

I like Jake and Maria, they often stick up for me. Jake's very good at PPF, even though he shouts out in class, and Maria does the high jump at athletics club. She's so good she represented Brazil.

I sat down at the back of the class and refreshed my mobile for the speech. I knew it off by heart but liked reading it over and over again. It distracted me from the talking that goes on during lessons when the teacher is speaking. The class is extra noisy for Mr Carter who speaks extra loudly in a slow, croaky voice, even though the geography class is small, only 15 children.

Suddenly, it was my turn to present. I took the yam out of my bag and I could hear someone laughing but I didn't know why. I stood up, scrolled down my mobile for the prompt list and took a deep breath like I was going to push out of the blocks for the 100 metres.

'Toomanycowsintheworldeatpeople.'

The whole class laughed so loud I couldn't rearrange my thoughts properly. That wasn't what I wanted to say but we were advised to deliver from prompts rather than read the full speech from the page. Mr Carter said we could use our mobile phones and make a list of words so we knew what to focus on for each section. My list said:

COWS
DAIRY
FISH
VEGETABLES

Looking at the word COWS had made me say cows first, when I should have said people. I'd memorised my speech word for word; I could see it in my mind, but my mouth mixed everything up and it came out like a long sentence in German that's all one word. I love German but not when I want to speak English. Mr Carter cleared his throat like he was starting a car on a cold day. He does everything in slow motion because he's older than Grandma. But before he could say anything at all, Pete LMS said, in my voice: 'MAD cows.'

Everyone laughed except Maria, who shouted across the room: 'Just cos you're Pete LMS doesn't mean we like you.'

Maria has hated Pete LMS since he wasn't picked for the athletics team and said high jump was only for freaks. Pete LMS makes fun of people who are different, especially if they're good at something. He calls Ben a Leaper after Big Ben let slip he was born on the 29th of February. Pete LMS doesn't know everyone in this school is a Leapling with The Gift. When we do PPF, he does history on his own.

I went from 0 to 10 in 0.5 seconds. I felt tears coming into my eyes and my face going red, even though I'm black and it doesn't show. But I had to do my speech. If I didn't do my speech, I'd get into trouble.

I stared down at my phone, the word COWS, and began again.

'Too many people in the world eat cows. They are addicted to burgers.'

'Ever seen a cow eat a burger?' shouted Pete LMS and banged his fist on the table. Everyone was laughing now, even Jake and Maria. But that wasn't what I meant. I meant PEOPLE are addicted to burgers.

I tried to continue my speech but every time I started a sentence Pete LMS would say the opposite and roll his eyes clockwise while Mr Carter looked out of the window because he's 103. Pete LMS gave me a hard time because his dad's a millionaire factory farmer who specialises in cattle, so if no one bought meat his whole family would starve. Actually, they wouldn't starve; they could eat the meat other people didn't buy. They'd be eating forever!

When I got to the FISH section, I looked down so I'd say the right words in the right order and noticed my screen was flashing. I had a text. In capital letters, it said:

SOS L

Sent Tue 3 Mar 2048. 23:00.

2048! It must be a mistake. I didn't recognise the number and I had lots of thoughts in my head at the same time. I closed my eyes and opened them again because the thoughts were coming too fast, one on top of the other, and maybe if I closed my eyes and opened them everything would be normal and I could carry on doing my speech. But when I opened my eyes, the thoughts kept coming like this:

SOS L

Who sent it? Why did they text ME?

SOS means someone's in trouble.

Howdidtheygetmynumber?

This isn't supposed to happen.

What does L mean? Is it a person who ends their texts with the initial L?

L means 50 in Roman numerals.

Is it someone pretending to be L to humiliate me? Like Pete LMS. Does he sign texts as L? But he's not a Leapling, how could he send a text from the future?

SOS means someone's in trouble!

It was sent in 2048 so it hasn't happened yet.

If you get a text about something that's GOING to happen, it's a Predictive.

SOS L is a Predictive!

Sent Tuesday the 3rd of March 2048, 11 o'clock at night.

2048 is the year of the school trip.

Maybe I can stop the bad thing that's going to happen.

I thought all this in ten seconds till I realised someone was nudging my hand. Suddenly, Pete LMS had my phone! He smiled like it was his birthday and this was the present he'd wanted for ages.

'SOS L,' he said, in my voice, to the whole class. Then, in his voice, 'A message from your Leaper boyfriend.'

I had a shooting pain in my head but I rushed across the room to get it back. I lunged towards Pete LMS and he laughed in my face. He was holding the phone too tight for me to grab it. Of course Mr Carter was a minute behind. Before he could say anything, Pete LMS said: 'Is The Palindrome about to cry? Boohoo!'

'That will be quite enough, Peter,' said Mr Carter in his slow, croaky voice.

Pete LMS stood up at his desk.

'Enough? I've had enough! Expect us to believe all this rubbish about man-made climate change?' We all gasped. 'My dad says Nature does what she likes. Nothing to do with man.'

He turned and threw my phone across the room. It crashed to the floor and the back came off.

And what did Mr Carter do? Continued the lesson, in his own time, like nothing had happened. His droning voice went on and on but it sounded like it was in the distance.

'Where are you going, Elle?'

I hadn't realised I'd packed my phone and yam, stood up, put my bag on my back, walked over to the door and opened it. Run round the track, I told myself. Do ten laps of the track. But instead I stood in the yellow corridor with all the thoughts spinning round my head. I closed my eyes, my body went fizzy and I leapt through time.

SOS L

Someone's in trouble in 2048 and I have to save them.

Chapter 03:00

MC^2

At the beginning of Seventh Year, a criminal came to our school. He was a skinny black boy with clumps of hair sticking out of his head like antennae. His eyes turned up at the edges and he had an infinity tattoo on his left hand which looked like a number 8 sideways: ∞. He wasn't in school uniform because he was a criminal, so his trousers and top were white with graffiti all over them. I tried to read what it said but it gave me a headache. His name was MC^2, the boy we'd see months later in the Time Squad video. But we didn't know that at the time.

Mrs C Eckler had given us investigative homework on MC^2 the night before, so we could ask sensible questions. She gave us a 'secret link' and reminded us of our Oath of Secrecy. That's when I found out he was a Leapling who'd committed lots of Anachronisms. Normal bad people commit crimes in their own time, but bad Leaplings steal things or kill people in the past so it's harder to trace the crime. All these crimes are called

Anachronisms. MC^2 was nicknamed the Mixer of Chronology but I didn't have time to find out what it meant because Grandma wanted me to fetch the comb and pomade.

Mrs C Eckler smelled of perfume that day rather than Pears soap. She had her ginger hair down to her shoulders rather than piled up on her head as usual and was wearing bright blue eyeshadow. I didn't like this. I kept thinking she was someone else who'd stolen Mrs C Eckler's voice.

'Now Seventh Year, we are EXTREMELY lucky today.' She was pacing up and down rather than standing still, which was really distracting. 'We have a very special visitor . . .' I think I zoned out during her introduction, but the next thing I knew everyone was cheering like he was a pop star.

MC^2 blinked all the time. He blinked so fast you might not even notice. I think he was scared. I tried to hate him because he'd broken the law but I felt bad for him because he was scared. And he spoke in rhyme so it was more like a rap than a talk.

> 'To the power of 2, I deliver my apology,
> I committed intricate crimes against chronology . . .'

That word again. Chronology. I know now it means the order that things happen. MC^2 was nicknamed the Mixer of Chronology because he sold things that were out of time, like DJs who used to 'mash up records' so the words came out backwards and sounded like another language. But I didn't know that last year.

'The making of watches and clocks is horology,
I stole the past, so the present acknowledge me.'

And I remembered reading online he became an expert on clocks and watches. He would go back in time to find a clock that was worth lots of money and then bring it back to the present to sell it. Then he did the opposite: he stole modern watches and sold them to rich people in the past. He didn't make as much money that way round but liked to watch people do what-big-eyes in 1800. The wristwatch hadn't been invented yet.

'If you're in a mess, if you're in distress,
send an SOS via SMS . . .'

Lots more applause.

And Mrs C Eckler was smiling from East to West.

'Thank you for that wonderful presentation, MC^2. Seventh Year have looked you up online so I'm sure they have lots of questions to ask you. But before they do, could you tell us the story of your name?'

'Yeah.' He disappeared, reappeared on the spot, his whole body blinking! Big Ben whooped, the whole class started muttering in amazement and my eyes went too big for my head. It was like leaping for a split second. How did he do it? 'When I was a kid,' he said, 'I leapt before I could walk. For real. Too much energy with no place to go. Doc said ADHD and prescribed medication. But the meds didn't work so I got sent specialist school to help me.'

'One of my peer mentors said,

"You're a bomb ready to blast, spar.
Channel that energy, you'll go far."

'I put my energy into rhyme. When I started rapping, I leapt all over the stage. Here, there, everywhere. There was this brother called himself Einstein after the genius professor that hatched nuclear energy. Einstein said, "You ain't just MC, you're MC^2." He didn't just mean a rapping MC. He named me after the formula: $E=MC^2$. E's Energy, M's mass, C's the speed of light. The most hyper MC on the planet.'

I've heard of the original Einstein. He had the best rhyming name ever. He wasn't a Leapling with The Gift but he must have had one in his family to get that surname. MC^2 is a brilliant name because it means lots of different things at the same time.

Mrs C Eckler thanked MC^2.

'Now Seventh Year, I know you have lots of questions.'

I put my hand up immediately and she peered round the room. 'Yes, Elle.'

I stood up. 'Doesn't MC also mean Mixer of Chronology? That's what it said online. And Master of Ceremonies?'

'Yeah. Maestro. Elle, isn't it? And Microphone Commando in hip hop and any other meaning you wannit to mean,' he said. 'I don't wanna confuse no one. But words are my specialisation. I like what they can do.'

'If you're a criminal, you are a liar because you don't want to get caught. So you could be lying to us now.'

I sat down, embarrassed. That didn't come out the way I wanted. I was happy and scared at the same time. I loved the way he made words sound like music but I didn't trust him. He was a criminal. He must have told lies to escape the police.

'I ain't a crim no more, Elle. An' I never told lies. When they caught me, I told the truth. I had to go back in time and replace everythin' I'd stolen so I didn't mess up history and vice versa.'

By messing up history, he meant you had to be careful when you went back in the past in case you swatted a fly and Hitler ended up winning World War Two. We did that in Sixth Year. I stood up again.

'Is it a poem about vices like greed and gluttony?' My voice was speaking before I could stop it.

'No.' He blinked. 'Vice versa's same as the other way round. I also had to find all the watches I'd sold in the past and bring them back to the present.'

'Did you kill anyone?'

Mrs C Eckler brought her eyebrows down to her eyes. I think she was cross. But I had to know whether he was bad or mega bad. He smiled.

'Never killed no one. Live by the knife, die by the knife.'

I remember wishing he didn't talk in riddles. What had knives got to do with it if he never killed anybody? Big Ben put his hand up.

'If you killed your dad in the past, will you die?'

'As I said . . .' He scrunched up his eyebrows. 'I never killed no one. But you're right. You wouldn't exist if you killed your dad. Your dad wouldn't meet your mum and hatch you. It would be a time paradox. Heard of the Grandfather Paradox? Same thing. Don't think it's ever happened.' He looked at Mrs C Eckler, who cleared her throat.

'Could you say something about the work you do NOW?'

But before MC^2 had time to respond, Jake said: 'Did you ever steal watches from the future?'

Trust Jake to ask this. He's always in trouble and I think he was asking for criminal tips rather than to learn from someone else's mistakes.

'Yes and no.' More riddles. 'I committed crimes but my action's bin erased. The future ain't fixed like the past. You can change it.'

I liked that idea. If you do something stupid in the future, you get another chance and another and another to make it right. You get an infinite amount of chances until it becomes the present. Then it's the past and you can't change it any more.

I think MC^2 liked that idea as well. He seemed to double in size.

'Now,' he said, like he was punching a hole in the present, 'I work for the Time Squad.'

I heard someone whisper, 'Thought it was the Rhyme Squad,' and Mrs C Eckler turned her head but she couldn't see who it was.

'We fight crime on the time-line. Mostly respond to SOS texts,' he continued. 'SOS is code for HELP. If an Anachronism's bin committed, usually someone's bin attacked or their life's in danger. We get there ASAP. Most texts come from the future.'

'Why?' Jake again. There's no hope for that boy.

'There's bin an upsurge of eco-crimes since the millennium. Peeps starting to realise they can make big cash from it. Easier to hide stuff in the future. You don't mess up history; you're less likely to get caught. Mostly smuggling. Meat, ivory, extinct animals. Toxic waste. The odd murder. Murderers get life imprisonment. Ad infinitum. Don't mean 20 years, means you're locked up till you drop down dead an' they bury you in the prison vaults.'

We all did what-big-eyes.

'How can you work in that job when you used to be a criminal?' Maria, and she didn't put her hand up. Sometimes she goes out of turn in a high jump competition, gets disqualified and swears in Portuguese. She hates rules.

'They gave me a choice.' He looked round the room and everyone was holding their breath to see what he'd say next. 'Work for us or go Young Offenders Unit. I made the right choice.'

I stood up. 'How old are you?' Mrs C Eckler gave me another look.

'15. And a bit. Lost count on my travels.'

We gasped. You're supposed to stay in full-time education till you're 18.

'I'm based in 2048. Different rules. If ya got talent, age don't matter.'

Mrs C Eckler cleared her throat as if to make an announcement. 'In Term four, there'll be a Leapling trip to 2048 where you'll have the chance to stay at the Time Squad Centre.' Class noise. 'It will be the last opportunity before it moves years. As you know, *the future is always in flux*. But we can only take four pupils. You have to earn it. I'll be assessing you on Effort the next two terms and make a selection based on that.' It all went quiet. There's fourteen of us. 'Yes, Ben.'

A three-second pause. Big Ben often pauses if you ask him a question, like he's translating it into English. It's the autism. You need to give him time to process. 'If you wanted to report a crime . . .' He paused again. 'An Anachronism. What number do we text?'

MC^2 scrunched his eyebrows again. '2000,' he said. 'Easy to remember. But text me now, an' your names, so you got Time Squad number on your memory. An' I got yours.' He took a massive silver phone out of his bag. 'If you come next year, you'll get a Chronophone. Can text past, present, future. Your TwentyTwenties should work normal.'

Mrs C Eckler gave him another mega smile. 'It's usually against school rules to use phones in lessons but this is a very special occasion. Please do as MC^2 says.'

I took out my phone, which is white, and renamed it TwentyTwenty in my head because I liked the echo, typed Time Squad and the number 2000. Then my name, letter by letter: E L L E and pressed send.

I could see Big Ben wanted to ask another question but he didn't put up his hand. He sounded like he was going to cough. But Mrs C Eckler could see as well and encouraged Big Ben to speak.

'If you got a Predictive, will you die?'

Mrs C Eckler cleared her throat. MC^2 stopped blinking and raised his eyebrows at Ben.

'Leap's done his homework,' he said. 'Predictives are rare, bro. VERY rare. You won't die. Depends on context, not TEXT. Know what a Predictive is?'

There was a long pause before Big Ben answered.

'When your phone sends a text before it happens.'

'Close. But it's not your phone. Someone types a text in the future to the past. Often a call for help. You get one, you gotta act on it.'

He looked at Big Ben for a long time before he nodded his head and smiled. Mrs C Eckler was looking at her watch.

'MC^2 is available to sign autographs afterwards and you'll have the chance to ask him a question 1-2-1, if you didn't get a chance just now.'

I didn't get his autograph. And I definitely didn't want to talk 1-2-1 with a criminal. It was noisy and I needed to go outside. Walking across the quad, I got out my phone and already there was a message from Time Squad:

MC^2.

∞ Chapter 04:00 ∞

OOPS

It's Thursday. I'm not going to school today. I'm tongue-tied.

Tongue-tied's not the same as not talking. Tongue-tied feels like someone's tied up your tongue so you can't talk. Not talking's when you could talk but choose to stay silent.

This might SOUND like talking but it's thoughts in my head.

Sometimes I think like I talk and things make sense.

Sometimes I talk like I think and my teachers say, 'Elle, have you swallowed a dictionary?' and I feel embarrassed.

And sometimes when my feelings get jumbled up my words get jumbled up too.

Or words come out in the wrong order or on top of each other.

Or I don't talk at all.

That's when under the table is the best place to be.

Today, I'm living under the table.

Though the table's higher than average, I have to bend my head down, so after a while my neck gets sore. It's hard to sit still under the table for long. Sometimes I lie down just to stretch out. I used to like living in my bed when I felt too many emotions at once, and noises went louder and smells went stronger and I needed somewhere quiet and calm to make the panic go away, but it was difficult to keep the sheet over my head. The table is better; the white cloth hangs right down to the floor all the way round. Like being in a tent. I love that. Last year I went camping with the school and it was perfect having my own tent to sleep in. It felt like my own little house. I was SO happy.

But today I'm angry and sad. I can cope with being sad, angry and scared, although I don't like it. But sometimes they get mixed up, like being happy and sad and scared at the same time. Yesterday I felt happy because leaping was like doing the long jump but ten times more exciting; sad because I leapt by mistake and if I had done it on purpose I would have gone backwards to make the bad thing unhappen, NOT forwards; scared because it's illegal to leap solo before you're 3-leap so I might get arrested and sent to a Young Offenders Unit.

Today I'm even tongue-tied with Grandma. I cooked her pepper soup for breakfast with yam and fish because she's Nigerian and her leg is paining her. She has rheumatoid arthritis. I looked it up on the internet. I don't think you can die from it but some mornings she's in so much pain she can't talk.

She wasn't talking this morning and she ate her pepper soup

sitting up in bed. She wrapped a white cardigan round her head as a headtie so she could bless the food in silence. When she prays over food she looks like she's warming her hands and she closes her eyes so tight they look like belly buttons. This morning I let Grandma squeeze my hand, which shows she liked the pepper soup. Sometimes she complains I didn't season it well, but today was the hand squeeze.

I ate mine at the table. I enjoyed it because it was a white meal. Yam is white unless it's yellow. Yellow yam is much more expensive so we never buy it. I like yam, even though it doesn't taste of anything. It has a creamy, grainy texture. Texture is the best part of food. Fish is white unless it's red. We only buy white fish. The fish is nice and flaky in my mouth.

The Pastor's wife smuggles yam from Nigeria in her suitcase and sells it on the Black Market. I used to think the Black Market was a market for black people, because white people eat potatoes and black people eat yam. Last time the Pastor's wife visited, the handle came off her suitcase walking up the stairs because yam is much heavier than potato. It looks like tree bark. I cut off the skin, which is tough work, and washed it in salt water to get rid of the starch. Then I boiled it and added it to the pepper soup at the last minute to soak up the flavour. I always take my yam out of the pepper soup and put coconut oil on it and mash it up. You're supposed to add palm oil but that's red or orange and messes up the rainforest. I take the fish out, too. Mashed yam and white fish is my favourite breakfast.

Afterwards, I cleared the table and collected Grandma's tray, washed the dishes and sat under the table. I've got my tablet and my mobile phone if I want to watch something or look something up. It's not very comfortable under the table but my hair is spongey, so it stops me banging my head on the wood. Today it's in bunches like ears on each side of my head. If I spend the whole morning here, when I come out to make lunch I'll feel happy.

∞

Someone's knocking on the front door.

We live on the first floor so we never answer the door. We'd rather have a ground-floor flat because Grandma struggles with the stairs but Mrs Leggett's lived downstairs for 30 years and refuses to die so no one else can rent her flat. There used to be a doorbell but it broke and the landlord won't fix it, so you have to knock. Some people knock so loud I think the door's going to cave in.

I'm sitting under the table, looking at the menu and the list of names for the trip. I'm going to be banned from the trip. I'm going to be excluded for running out of a lesson and leaping out of school and sprinting away from Mrs C Eckler, but that doesn't stop me looking at the list of names. I like lists. Lists are like poems. Lists help me stay calm.

I'm looking at the list of names so I can imagine what the people are like and don't have to think about SOS L and running out of a lesson and being excluded. And not being able to go on Leap 2048. I've never run out of a lesson before so I'll definitely be excluded. But Grandma would be horrified if I was excluded because I have good grades in every subject. I would be horrified too.

They gave us a list of all the pupils on the trip so we can make friends more quickly when we get there. They have the same details so they know about us too. Half the pupils are Annuals from 2048 who've sworn the Oath of Secrecy because they have a Leapling with The Gift in their family.

Name	Age on 29 February	Leap Year	School/ Institution
Ama Atta Asante	14	2048	Music, Maths and Movement
Seren Thomas	13	2048	Music, Maths and Movement
Megan Smith	13	2048	Music, Maths and Movement
Yusuf Ali	15	2048	Music, Maths and Movement
Martin Aston	13	2048	E-College-E
Kate Loftis	12	2048	E-College-E
Ben Novak	12	2020	Intercalary International
Jake Bartholomew	12	2020	Intercalary International
Elle Ifíè	12	2020	Intercalary International

Maria de Santos	12	2020	Intercalary International
GMT	16	1968	Home School
Noon McFarland	16	1924	Governess

I'm really looking forward to meeting Noon McFarland because her name is a palindrome like mine but is extra cool because if you write it in capital letters, NOON, it reads EXACTLY the same upside down AND refers to time. She was taught at home with a governess, which is like a tutor who comes to your house and is very strict. She's 16 but Mrs C Eckler said she might seem younger than 16-year-olds nowadays because she hasn't been allowed out very much. And because she won't be used to things like hairdryers and mobile phones we have to help her adapt.

I can't wait to meet GMT because she goes to Home School, which means her parents teach her at home, and comes from 1968, so she may have met Bob Beamon at the 1968 Olympic Games in Mexico City. But if she's travelling from February 1968 the Olympics wouldn't have started yet. The 1968 Olympics were held in October because it's so hot in Mexico people would have died of heatstroke if they'd held them in August. But it was high altitude, so runners were flopping down like limp lettuce. There wasn't enough oxygen.

I'll be sharing a chalet with Noon and GMT and Ama. Mrs C Eckler says they mixed the ages so some of the older ones can mentor the younger ones, except Noon, who might need mentoring herself. GMT is also 16 and Ama is 14, which is good because I find it easier to talk to people older or a lot younger than me. Big Ben's the main person my age I speak to. Ama goes to the Music, Maths and Movement School. In 2048, children go to schools depending on what they're good at. The E-College-E pupils are good at biology and geography and conflict resolution.

I'm excited to meet all these new people but scared because I haven't met them before. Mrs C Eckler showed us everyone's photos so I know what they look like. I always remember what I see. Noon has short blonde hair in a bob and big starey eyes; GMT has tanned skin and long black straggly hair that looks like she never combs it; and Ama has a huge ginger afro and a gap in the middle of her teeth. Ama's going to be my mentor for the week. Big Ben has to share with Jake and two other boys he doesn't know. He doesn't like meeting new people and he finds boys harder to talk to than girls. But he liked looking at the photos of the boys and he's excited about the trip. One of them's called Martin Aston, which is Aston Martin the other way round. I hope he's into cars.

I like looking at the list and imagining what the other girls will be like and then I remember I'm going to be excluded and will never meet them anyway. I've never been excluded before but I've had several red cards and been sent to the Head Teacher lots. I don't know why they use red cards because school isn't a football match, it's learning. When it's meltdown, and I go from 0 to 10, the last thing I need is a red card. They should give me a white card. A white card would calm me down but a red card makes me dizzy and scared.

The last time I went to the Head was when I hid under the table during maths because Joanne Fletcher was sitting in my seat and told me to get over it, and Mrs Grayling grabbed me by the hands to pull me back to my seat so I could finish my algebra and I wanted to hit her but couldn't because I'd get excluded if I hit a teacher so I started to scream until they had to get Mrs C Eckler to calm me down.

I'm thinking this when the knocking on the door gets much louder, like the person is angry. Why doesn't Mrs Leggett open it? Who could be visiting at this time of day? Maybe someone has come to see Grandma. I remember the phone rang several times this morning and I didn't answer it. My mobile buzzed and I ignored it in case it was another Predictive.

I think about ignoring the door but Grandma shouts from the bedroom.

'Elle, answer the door. Answer it-o! I'm expecting the Pastor.'

The Pastor sometimes comes to pray over Grandma's leg to make the pain go away. But it may not be the Pastor. It could be the Leap Police, who've come to arrest me for my illegal leap.

'Elle, rise from this your table before my ears bust. Please, I beg!'

Even if it's the Police I have to go downstairs and answer the door. But it isn't the Police with steel handcuffs, or the Pastor smelling of palm oil. It's Mrs C Eckler.

'Can I come in, Elle?' she says. I don't know why she's asking, as she's already walking up the stairs and entering our flat. I close the door and take a deep breath.

Either she's come to exclude me for running out of class without time-out permission or for running away from her car. Time-out permission is when I'm allowed to leave class to do running round the track. I couldn't ask for time-out permission yesterday because my voice stopped working and my legs wanted to run home rather than round the track but I ended up leaping instead. I hope she doesn't know about THAT.

She's looking around the room and I feel ashamed of the damp patch that grows mushrooms on the wall behind the television. The mushrooms are grey and look like ears you've scrunched up in your hands. I don't know what kind of mushrooms they are, but I bet they have a long name in Latin and if you eat them you'll die. Even though I cut them down and scrub the patch every Saturday, they never really go away. Mrs C Eckler is turning her head, looking like she's lost something.

'Is your grandmother here?'

I point towards the bedroom door and, at the same time, Grandma says, 'Elle, who is here?'

I open the bedroom door and Mrs C Eckler follows me into the bedroom. I'm not happy. No one gave her permission to enter the bedroom. Does she think she owns the flat? But Grandma is sitting up in bed, now wearing her yellow-and-blue fish headtie and smiling.

'Mrs Eckler, you are welcome. Please. Take a seat.'

Grandma missed out the C but I don't think Mrs C Eckler is offended. No one knows what the C stands for. Some people think it's Carol but I have a better idea. I think it stands for 100 because C is 100 in Roman numerals.

I don't know why Grandma is pleased to see Mrs C Eckler. I'm about to be excluded from Intercalary International. Grandma extends her hand to Mrs C Eckler and says, 'I am very pleased with the progress Elle is making in her PPF.'

I'm a Level 4, which is almost the equivalent of GCSE level, exceptional for a Seventh Year. I'm pleased Grandma is pleased, but I don't think she knows what PPF really is. Grandma never learnt to read and write. Even though she can't read herself and does know what it's about, she won't let me read Harry Potter because 'na full of witchcrafts'. She doesn't understand there are good witchcrafts and bad witchcrafts. Harry Potter is about good overcoming evil.

'Yes, Mrs Ifíè. We are very proud of Elle. She is a clever girl. But . . .'

She pauses and I hold my breath. I know what she's going to say.

'Elle has been bullied by one of the other children. We take bullying very seriously at Intercalary International.'

My mouth falls open in a capital O for Oops. This is not what I was expecting. Even though it's a good surprise, I still find it difficult to cope with the change. If I was talking, this would make me tongue-tied. But as I'm already tongue-tied, my heart beats fast like it wants to jump out of my chest. For a moment, I feel so panicked I wish Mrs C Eckler had excluded me. Big Ben says Oops is like when you drive your car five miles down a narrow country lane then suddenly have to reverse because a tractor's coming from the opposite direction. Reversing back to the junction's much harder than driving forwards. You could turn the steering wheel the wrong way and end up in a ditch.

Grandma is now sitting up in bed but I can tell she is in a lot of pain because her eyes are still scrunched like she's just woken up. She looks at Mrs C Eckler, then at me.

'On the seventh day, God took rest. Not the fourth.' Her eyes go big as Jupiter. 'Elle, why are you not in school?'

Mrs C Eckler speaks quickly.

'Elle has been granted some time off while we deal with the bullying.'

Mrs C Eckler is lying. No one gave me permission to stay off school, but I'm still not talking so I don't say anything. Grandma doesn't understand bullying. At the age of 12, she had left school and was looking after her younger brothers and sisters in the village in Nigeria. But she always wished she'd studied longer so she could read and write. She worships teachers almost as much as God. If Mrs C Eckler says I can stay at home, then Grandma is happy. She smiles from her bed.

'Elle, make this your teacher a cup of tea.'

I go to the kitchen to boil the kettle but can hear everything Mrs C Eckler is saying, how all the speeches were recorded so they have the bullying on record, how the bully has been excluded for a week, how she's going to put me on a special support programme after the school trip. AFTER the trip. So I'm still allowed to go. I'm happy until I remember I don't want to go because the Predictive means someone's in danger and I have to save them and I don't know how. But at the same time I want to go because I've been looking forward to this trip for weeks. I pour the boiling water into the mug and add the evaporated milk and one sugar. That's how I like it.

When I go back into the bedroom, Mrs C Eckler sips the tea and makes a face like it's too hot. But I added loads of milk, so it can't be.

'Elle, are you happy about going on the Leap 2048 trip?'

I lower my eyes. I can't lie. But I can't tell Mrs C Eckler about the Predictive. Now that I'm not excluded, and I'm allowed to go, I really don't want to. I'm scared. I shake my head. Grandma addresses Mrs C Eckler.

'She refuses to talk. What for? Even last night she could not say Amen after evening prayer. What evil spirit is possessing her?' She kisses her teeth.

Mrs C Eckler is facing Grandma but she says, 'Elle, I think you're not talking because the bully has threatened you. But don't worry. They will be punished.'

I smile. Mrs C Eckler is kind but she doesn't understand the real reason I'm not talking. It wasn't the bullying; it was the bullying plus the text message. Events were one on top of the other, like words that are impossible to read. I can't tell her.

She continues, still looking at Grandma because she knows I don't like it when people stare at me, 'But Leap 2048 is special and you are my star pupil. It's the chance of a lifetime. There will never be another opportunity to make that leap.'

She says the next bit to Grandma.

'This trip will be good for Elle's confidence. The future is better for Leaplings like Elle. I've seen them thrive.' She pauses.

'Elle has formal permission to stay at home tomorrow . . .' She produces some forms for Grandma to sign. As if Grandma can read what they say. They could say anything, like Elle will be executed tomorrow, and Grandma would still sign them for Mrs C Eckler. 'I can collect you here at 5:45 on Saturday morning. What do you say?'

I'm still looking at the floor when I'm aware Grandma is facing me. I can almost feel the steam coming off her, the force of her all-the-better-to-see-you-with-eyes, like the wolf in *Red Riding Hood*.

'Elle Bíbi-Imbelé Ifíè! Did I not teach you? *Do unto others as you would have them do unto you.* Mrs C Eckler is helping you. You must help her back. She has arranged a trip for you. It is your duty to attend.'

She slumps back into the bed like a toy that's run out of batteries. I was raised to respect my elders and I've never disobeyed Grandma before, apart from reading Harry Potter.

Mrs C Eckler looks at me for the first time in minutes. I'm thinking about the quote. *Do unto others as you would have them do unto you*. I want to help Mrs C Eckler but I'm also thinking about SOS L. If someone IS in trouble, it's my duty to help them.

Bob Beamon had two fouls before he got through to the Olympic final in 1968. He kept jumping over the board. His teammate told him to change his run-up so he could take off on his right foot and he jumped 2 feet before the board and managed to make it through to the final. 8 metres 90 was his first jump in the final. If his teammate hadn't helped him, he would never have had the chance to make his record-breaking jump.

Mrs C Eckler is helping me like a teammate.

I make sure Mrs C Eckler is watching before I nod my head. And she smiles.

Chapter 05:00

LEAP 2048

Today is the 29th of February 2020. My birthday! I'm 3-leap. 12 years old! And I'm going to 2048!

I sit up on the sofa and find my phone. I sleep on the sofa because we only have one bedroom and Grandma snores. Not that I slept much last night. I stayed up till midnight so I could be awake for the first minute of my birthday. Then I went to sleep but kept waking up. My head was throbbing because Grandma cornrowed my hair into four rows, tight enough to last the week. When I arrive, I'll take it out and put it in bunches. I prefer it like that even though I have to plait it every night. I hope I sleep better in 2048. Last night, I heard the clock tower chime every hour on the hour.

I check my phone to see if I have any messages before the trip. Mrs C Eckler said we're allowed to bring our phones but they might not work in 2048. We'll be allocated Chronophones when we arrive. They can send messages across time: past, present and future. I haven't had any more messages since the

Predictive. I look at the message for one last time, then delete it. It's in my mind with all the details: Sent Tue 3 Mar 2048. 23:00. As soon as I've deleted it I regret it, but I'm scared that if a grown-up finds my phone I'll get into trouble. It's not lying but you might call it destroying the evidence.

Even if something's deleted, it still happened.

Grandma's shuffling around in the bedroom. She always wakes up early to pray and I know she wants to pray with me before I go. She made white moi-moi for me to have for breakfast and take on the trip. Moi-moi is made from black-eyed beans, but when you soak them the skin comes off, so only the white beans are ground up. It's usually orange when cooked because you add stew made of pureed onions and tomatoes but, for me, Grandma just put onions and seasoning in it. It's not white; it's grey, but still colourless and yummy.

My suitcase is so heavy I can hardly lift it off the floor, but Mrs C Eckler will help me carry it. It's heavy because I've taken some yams. I don't think they'll have yams in 2048 and I eat yam every day so want to have enough. Mrs C Eckler said I was allowed to take some of my favourite foods because of my sensory issues. Big Ben will be pleased because his favourite food is spicy, so I said I would make him some pepper soup.

Grandma has reached the section of the prayer where she asks for my safe transport when my phone buzzes and I realise Mrs C Eckler has arrived. Grandma's eyes are closed so I have to interrupt.

'Grandma, Mrs C Eckler is here.'

She talks over me until she finishes the prayer with the words, 'Elle, answer the door!'

I obey. I didn't know she heard me. Maybe I didn't say it out loud, only in my head. I haven't spoken aloud for two days. I tiptoe downstairs, as we mustn't wake the other tenants this early. Mrs C Eckler is with her husband, who's coming on the trip to help. He's a Leapling as well. Leaplings often marry each other because it makes it easier to go on holiday together. I don't know whether to call him Mr Eckler or Mr C Eckler. I decide not to speak to him directly.

Mrs C Eckler has her ginger hair piled high on her head as usual but a large white flower pinned on the left-hand side. Her husband is very tall and is wearing sunglasses. In February! He carries my suitcase down the stairs like it weighs nothing. Grandma insists on hobbling after him so she can see me off outside. She breathes out heavily with each step and I worry she might struggle to get back up again. She hugs me so hard I can't breathe but I like that much more than when she squeezes my hand. Then she turns back into the house and I get into the back of Mrs C Eckler's bright red Audi Ur-Quattro.

Big Ben says it's too old to go properly fast, but I like it. Mrs C Eckler says it was made in 1984, which was the year she was born, and it was a birthday present from her husband four years ago. I've been in it before when I've had to go home from school in the middle of the day. I like old cars better than new ones, but Big Ben always likes the latest version of everything. He wants to design cars when he's a grown-up.

It's another cold day and still pitch black. We go the opposite route to the one I ran home. Mrs C Eckler drives. She won't let her husband drive the car, ever. She says it's hers, which is true. But she's not a very good driver, she goes 35 in a 30-miles-per-hour limit. That's illegal. Mr C Eckler has been given strict instructions. His job is to carry the suitcases out of the car to Block T once we reach the school. We must assemble in Room 4D, which is named after the fourth dimension, space–time. The other dimensions are height, breadth and depth. We never have PPF lessons in Room 4D. It's reserved exclusively for leaps.

∞

'Would anyone like a leap band?'

Leap bands are metal bangles you wear if you get leapsickness. I read about them on the itinerary. I'm glad Mrs C Eckler has brought them along because it might stop me vomiting like I did after my solo leap. She has leap bands in several different metals, gold, silver and bronze. They remind me of the medals in the Olympics, so I choose a gold one. Who would go for bronze?

We're sitting in a circle that goes like this, in a clockwise direction: me, Big Ben, Mr C Eckler, Maria, Jake, Mrs C Eckler. When you leap in a circle, it's called a Chrono. Six is a good number for an interdecade leap. When we hold hands, that's 12 hands representing each hour of the clock.

Mrs C Eckler makes sure we place all our luggage in the

middle of the circle otherwise it will get left behind and we'll spend the week with no clothes. I've heard Leaplings can transport Annuals like luggage but you need a very large Chrono for it to work. I check I have my phone in my pocket, even though I checked three times at home and twice in the back of the car. Most of the suitcases are black but mine is white, obviously. My suitcase is right in front of me. Mrs C Eckler stands up and we all go quiet.

'Thank you, everybody, for being on time.' She smiles like she's made a joke. 'As you all know, today is the 29th of February 2020, a very special day. It celebrates the way humans have allocated time. The 29th of February is made up of six hours from each of the four years, which equals 24 hours saved up and carried over to make an extra full calendar day each leap year. Today is vibrating with four years of energy. It's the best day to time travel. Happy Birthday to us all!'

Everyone claps and Big Ben punches the air rather than correct her maths. It's actually a bit less than six hours from each of the four years but the maths balances out in the end. We lose three leap days every 400 years. I'm glad I was born in 2008. It's lovely to be with other Leaplings on my birthday.

'We will be arriving at Time Squad Centre at 7 a.m. 2048,' Mrs C Eckler continues. 'We will be there seven days. We will return here at 3 o'clock on the 29th of February 2020. You will be able to celebrate your special birthday twice: once this evening in the future and once when you're back home.'

Mrs C Eckler looks around the circle. 'Any questions? Yes, Jake.'

'Is there breakfast when we arrive? I'm starving!'

'Yes. When we arrive, we go straight to The Beanstalk Café, where they will be serving breakfast.'

She looks around the circle again but no one else speaks. Big Ben, who usually asks questions in our PPF group, is squeezing my hand so hard I'm worried he'll break my fingers.

'OK. Come, let us link hands.'

It sounds like something Grandma would say, quoting from the Bible. I think that's what the first bissextiles said, when they discovered they had The Gift. Most gifted Leaplings find it difficult to leap alone and end up in the right place and time. You have to be really strong-minded, have intense powers of concentration and exceptional stamina. Maybe it helped that I was tongue-tied when I did it by mistake. I was able to concentrate to the max. But I still went forward in time instead of back.

This is my first time doing a group leap. My left hand holds Big Ben: my right, Mrs C Eckler. I suddenly realise it's not Big Ben squeezing my hand super tight; it's me squeezing his. I don't want him to think he's my boyfriend. My hands start to feel fizzy, like when I get a static shock taking washing out of the tumble dryer. Grandma can't manage the laundry, so I take it in the shopping trolley to the laundrette every week, and every time I get a shock. I hate that. This fizzing is worse because it doesn't stop, but Mrs C Eckler warned us about it and says it passes in about 30 seconds when the power reaches its height.

This is like my solo leap to the power of 6. That doesn't mean 6 x 1, it means 6 x 6 x 6 x 6 x 6 x 6. Big Ben taught me that. I don't feel like I'm in a car accelerating to top speed but staying in the same place. I AM the car. Big Ben's done an interdecade leap before and he loved it. He said it felt like being a Koenigsegg Agera RS. Not that he's ever even been in one. But he could imagine it. I feel sick. I close my eyes and squeeze both hands tighter. I'm scared. Scared I'm going to vomit. Then I remember what it said on the itinerary. If you feel sick, concentrate on the number. The number for our trip is the year of destination: 2048. I focus on 2048. 2048. 2048. The numbers work their magic. I think I hear Mrs C Eckler saying the number but I'm not sure whether it's her saying it now or me remembering her saying it in a lesson and it's playing back in my head. It sounds like a recording.

I relax. Though I still have my eyes closed, I can see everything's become brighter. It's like looking at a red screen rather than a black one. But it's not a plain red screen. If I look closely, I can see tiny grains of black right in the middle. Numbers. The first two numbers are two and zero and they don't change. But the last two are flickering like a countdown. Except it's a countup: 37, 38, 39. We reach 2040 and the numbers start to slow down. Almost there.

I'm too scared to open my eyes but I want to. This is hard. I squeeze Big Ben's hand and Mrs C Eckler's hand. No one's talking but they both squeeze my hands back. I concentrate on 2048. The numbers slow right down. I can feel light rain on my face and hear birds singing. I open my eyes.

We are no longer in Room 4D in Block T in Intercalary International.

We are outside the Time Squad Centre.

We must keep holding hands until Mrs C Eckler says we can stop.

I'm so excited I shout out loud inside my head.

Chapter 06:00

FERRARI FOREVER

'1 minute 59 seconds,' says Big Ben.

He was counting in his head and I bet he's right but it felt like half an hour. We're still holding hands. Mrs C Eckler told us we must maintain the energy to centre ourselves. I know if I move I'll be sick. The air is very warm for February, like the middle of summer. But the light rain is helping; it's good to be outside. We're in the eco play park, where everything's made of trees, and still looks like trees. If I didn't feel sick, I'd go on the swings.

I love swinging. Before school when I was in First Year, Grandma took me to the park every day to calm me down when my body felt fizzy. One morning I counted each swing up to 100 out loud and Grandma was crying because she was happy. I know that sounds odd, but she said they were tears of joy. I never used to talk very much and she didn't know I knew my numbers. Afterwards, she had to sit down on the bench to get her breath back.

Everywhere I look, there's trees. Some of them are like brown canes coming out of the ground with ruler marks on them. Mrs C Eckler sees me looking.

'They're bamboo, Elle. The fastest grow 90 centimetres a day!'

Some of the trees have trunks so large you could live in them. You could have one room on each floor and a spiral staircase going up. I think they're oak trees which are hundreds of years old. I'd love to live in a REAL treehouse. And there's palm trees too, lots of different kinds. It's the greenest place I've ever seen. Except for the glass building in the middle, which is the centre, it's like a tropical jungle. I wonder if they grow trees inside the centre, like in a glasshouse. That would be better than the pretend beanstalk in the café video. I could happily sit here forever if I didn't feel sick.

I can hear birds singing and a strange noise like the sound of a fast car approaching but it's like someone turned the sound of the engine off. Like the sound's invisible. And it's coming from the sky!

I slowly turn my head to see a lime-green car descending in front of the centre! It's so green it hurts my eyes, but I can't stop them staring in amazement. I've always been car blind; most cars look the same to me, but this is definitely a supercar. I never saw a flying car before, and certainly not a flying supercar. Big Ben lets go of my hand and starts shouting in noises rather than words, he's so excited. Big Ben can imitate different supercar noises brilliantly. His best impersonation is the Lamborghini Asterion but it's always so loud I put my hands over my ears. Now, I want to move my head to see what he's doing but if I move my head I'll vomit so I stay still. Mrs C Eckler squeezes my hand.

'Elle, are you OK?'

I'm scared to shake my head so I don't do or say anything. She squeezes my hand.

'Well done, everyone. That went smoothly. We've arrived at the centre. Stop linking hands now but remain seated. Heston,' that's her husband, 'keep an eye on Ben.'

I can hear Big Ben whooping in the background. He's not just happy, he's ecstatic. I feel like I'm going to die of nausea but very, very slowly turn my head in his direction. The lime-green supercar has parked in front of the main entrance. Big Ben is running up and down, whooping and flapping his hands. It's obviously a very special car. The driver's door opens but I don't see who gets out because, without warning, at that exact moment, I projectile vomit all over my suitcase.

∞

'Whatisitwhatisitwhatisitwhatisit?'

Big Ben's doing chanting and running around like an aeroplane. We're in The Beanstalk having breakfast. I stare at the huge green beanstalk in the middle of the room. It has grooves on it, like the bamboo, so that you can climb up if you want to. Jake's hanging off one of the top tendrils. Season, who runs the café, sees me put my hand over my mouth. I'm scared he'll fall.

'Don't worry,' she says. 'The floor's designed for spills and falls.'

There's only the six of us; no one else has arrived yet. Everything starts at 9 a.m. I've only just come in. I sat outside for half an hour and Season gave me a clear sweet to suck after I vomited.

'You'll be right as rain soon,' she said in a Scottish accent I didn't notice in the film, and she is fatter than I remembered. Why do people say right as rain? I hate rain, so how can it be right?

But she IS right. The rain made me feel refreshed and the sweet took away the nausea and Mr C Eckler took away my suitcase and Mrs C Eckler led me down into The Beanstalk. I like it in here. Everything's clean and white: the plates, the cups, the tables, the walls. Everything's gleaming. And though it's raining outside, the sun streams through all the glass, making everything sparkle. Light rain mixed with sunlight isn't drizzle, it's drazzle.

I sit eating a roll with some white paste in the middle. I'm not sure what it is, but I eat it anyway. The coconut water is heavenly. Big Ben's still doing his chanting and running when Season comes to sit with us.

'Feeling any better now?'

She smells of freshly baked bread. She has small hands with sparkly white nail polish. I remember her kneading bread in the film.

'Are you going to teach us to make bread?'

She smiles. 'I hope so. It's my . . . speciality.'

I like the way she emphasises the word 'speciality' by pausing before it. That's called a meaningful pause. I wonder if bread is her specialist subject.

'Are you autistic?'

'Yes, Elle. I'm a supertaster cook and call myself Autie-Auto at the car club.'

I LOVE her nickname and that she's into cars like Big Ben. She has the blackest, silveriest, shiniest hair imaginable, better than in the video, like a black-silver glass skyscraper on top of her head. She turns to Mrs C Eckler, who's sitting next to me in case I projectile vomit again.

'He's quite a character,' meaning Big Ben.

'He's car mad,' I say, and Season laughs. Her laugh sounds as glittery as her fingernails. Then she says something surprising.

'It's mine. If he's good this week, I can take him out for a . . .'

She's the opposite of Big Ben. He pauses before he speaks; Season pauses at the end of sentences. But I guess she was going to say 'ride'. Big Ben would love that. But I'm trying to get my head round what she said.

'How did you afford such an expensive car? I mean, you're a cook, you can't make much money.'

Mrs C Eckler brings her eyebrows down to her eyes, even though she told me she used to say rude things all the time when she was young. But Season isn't cross.

'My brother and I used to run a garage. When I decided to become a cook, we traded everything in for the Ferrari.'

Big Ben stops in his tracks and turns to our table. 'Whatisit? What is it?'

'A Ferrari Forever,' says Season. 'The most eco-friendly supercar. A wind-rain hybrid. We get a lot of both.' As if it heard her, the wind outside starts howling, lashing rain onto the glass roof of the café. Big Ben does his three-second pause.

'0 to 60?'

'1.4 seconds on land.'

Big Ben punches the air with both fists. I've never seen him so happy. If he knew Season would take him out for a ride, he'd die on the spot. Season tilts her head to one side and says, 'If you're good this week, I'll take you out for a flight.'

So 'flight' was the word, not 'ride'. I can see Big Ben's sad. His mouth turns down at the corners.

Pause. 'I don't want to fly; I want to drive.'

'OK. We can stay on the ground.' Season smiles.

'Wannadrivewannadrivewannadrive!' No pause at all.

'You're too young to drive, Ben, even in 2048. But, if you're good' – she stresses the word 'good' – 'I'll teach you the driverless three-point . . .'

She stops talking and stares across at the table where Jake is eating a bacon sandwich. That would be normal, except there's no bacon on the menu. I could smell it when he took it out of his bag, even though he must have made it hours ago, in 2020. I have an exceptional sense of smell. Season probably has too.

'Jake,' she says, and I'm surprised she has learnt all our names so quickly. 'Meat is forbidden on these premises. If you want to eat meat, you'll have to go outside.'

Jake clockwises his eyes. I know that's rude but I'm not surprised. Jake's always breaking the rules.

'Mum said not to eat before take-off, in case I threw up.'

'Did you not eat breakfast in here just now?'

'Yeah, I did.' He wriggles his nose. 'But bacon butties are better!'

Season looks cross.

'Next time, try the beancon. You won't taste the difference. You shouldn't have transported it. I should report it as an Anachronism but . . .' She shrugs her shoulders. 'It's not worth the paperwork.'

She addresses us all.

'If anyone else has meat with them, declare it now!'

There's total silence. Even Big Ben stops his wannadrive chant.

'OK. Let's go outside. And Ben,' she adds, 'I'm sure you want to see Fiona. Fiona the Ferrari!'

Everyone laughs. A car with its own name.

∞

Fiona has chocolate-brown vegan leather seats with white stitching and a matching steering wheel. I'm not into cars like Big Ben but even I think she's exceptional. Season lets Big Ben sit in the driving seat to pretend he's driving, then she lets Jake, once he's finished his sandwich.

'Would you like a go, Elle?'

I shake my head. It smells too much of baked plastic, and though I feel 95% I don't want to be sick again. Instead, I walk round the outside of the car and notice the wheels match the steering wheel. I've never seen chocolate-brown tyres before. I thought all tyres were black. The best bit is the number plate:

F1 0NA

I'm still admiring Fiona when I hear buzzing and look up. There are lots of black dots in the sky in formation like birds. When a bird formation moves around like a snake it's called a murmuration. I learnt that in science. I like the feel of the word murmuration in my mouth, even though I'm not speaking out loud. It could be birds, but maybe it's giant bees. It SOUNDS like bees.

Now everyone's looking up. Big Ben's mouth is a capital O. Some of the black dots have formed a murmuration of their own and they're heading for the centre. They're not birds, or bees. They're PEOPLE!

A light-skinned black girl with a huge ginger afro lands first. When her feet hit the ground, she runs fast for about 40 metres. Maybe she'll do sprint training with me. She's wearing a jacket with a shell on the back that makes her look like a giant insect. I recognise her from the photo: Ama, my mentor for the week. She waves over at us. She's followed by three other teenage girls and two boys who run 50 metres after they land. Yusuf and Martin. The E-College-E pupils must have flown with the Music, Maths and Movement School because they're all from 2048. One of the girls rushes over to the car with her mouth open. It's Seren. She must like cars as much as Big Ben! Season lets her sit inside as Ama comes over to me.

'Wreckage!' she says, looking at Fiona. Mrs C Eckler said in 2048 if something's perfect you say wreckage. So Ama must love the Ferrari.

'I'm Ama,' she says and holds out her hand.

'I'm Elle,' I say. 'How fast can you run the 100 metres?' I'm surprised that I'm talking to her without feeling scared. After all, I never met her in my life. I don't know what I'm supposed to do with her hand, so I ignore it. She shrugs.

'Ama means born on Saturday.'

'And it's a palindrome.' I smile. 'Is it your birthday today?'

'No,' she says. 'I'm not a Leapling, but my brother was.' She suddenly looks sad. 'Catch you later.'

She walks quickly to the main entrance. Two of the 2048 teachers, a fat man and a woman with purple hair, help the pupils take off their insect jackets, which are called eco-jets, and we all go inside. It's 8:55 a.m. The introductory session is about to begin and we must be on time. This is the Time Squad Centre after all!

As I walk inside, I notice a girl with short blonde hair sitting in the park and recognise her as Noon. She's wearing beige-cream two-tone shoes with a strap across the middle and heels shaped like an hourglass. She has all-the-better-to-see-you-with-eyes and I wait for a second or two to see if she's going to projectile vomit. If she does, I'll ask Season to give her a sweet. She stands up and I see that she's quite tall, taller than me in her shoes. She picks up her suitcase and walks slowly towards the entrance, looking down at the ground the whole time.

I follow Noon into the centre. Noon could become my friend instead of Ama. I don't know why I made Ama sad. I'm scared she won't ever want to be my friend. I wish I hadn't spoken to her now. Did I do or say something wrong? Maybe she doesn't like athletics. Maybe she wishes she was a Leapling. She said, 'I'm not a Leapling but my brother WAS.'

Maybe her brother is dead.

Chapter 07:00

NAMES

'Welcome to Leap 2048!

'Happy 3rd leap birthday to the Intercalary International pupils who've joined us from 2020. You have come of age.

'Happy 4th leap birthday to my colleague, MC^2. May you enjoy the privileges and responsibilities the age bestows upon you.

'Happy birthday to all bissextiles from other years.

'Welcome to the Annual pupils from Music, Maths and Movement, and E-College-E, who've joined us from the CURRENT year.'

Millennia, the centre director, is giving her welcome address. She looks taller and older than in the film, but maybe she's wearing platform shoes under her purple hooded gown and the film was made a while ago. She may have time-travelled for years between making the film and now. Who knows? Her hair, white and spiky, still looks like an electric shock. And though her face is lined like a cracked vase, she sounds lively when she speaks. Her voice is decades younger than her body.

'Today is the 29th of February 2048.

'This is the present.

'Whether you've travelled here from the present, the past or the future, enjoy the present moment, seize the day. *Carpe diem.*'

Millennia's like me. She likes words and the spaces between words. She speaks slowly and clearly like some teachers do so we can all follow everything she's saying. But when she got to the Latin words, she said them too loudly and I jumped. I don't trust people who make me jump. I don't listen to it all because she's talking for a very long time and I'm constantly distracted. Ama's sitting next to me and keeps whispering things like:

'She set up this centre in 2000 to fight time-crime,'

and

'No one knows how old she is. Def over 100!'

And I keep looking at the others on the stage with her, from left to right, like I'm reading words on a page. On the far left sits Season, then the criminal, MC^2, then Millennia, then Le Temps. When she introduces them, their names flash up on the screen behind and they remind me of something. I think it might be the video we saw in school but it's something else and I can't work it out.

I'm distracted by that and simultaneously thinking about how fast Ama can run the 100 metres because she didn't answer my question. Underneath all that, I'm thinking about SOS L, but I try to switch that thought off because I'm starting to go into overload. I look up at the glass dome on the ceiling. The sky is grey and it's still raining. I imagine rain spitting on my face like silver pins.

'We have few rules here but they are important ones:

'One. We are totally eco-friendly. By choice and necessity. You've been told that due to the meat rations most institutions have a meat-free policy. Here, we are meat-free apart from special festivals.

'Today is a special festival. Tonight, we will offer meat at the birthday barbecue, as well as a large range of vegan delicacies.'

Jake and a couple of the Triple Ms cheer. We call Music, Maths and Movement pupils Triple Ms because Music, Maths and Movement is a mouthful. The E-Cos, Martin and Kate, narrow their eyes at the mention of meat. They don't eat anything that has a heart, not even lettuce!

Millennia continues:

'Two. Age doesn't matter. Some of us are young but old beyond our years; some are old, but old people are simply young people who've lived longer; some are middle-aged and some have leapt so much they've lost count of the years. What matters is skill, wisdom . . .'

I don't know what Millennia is going to say next because suddenly, in the middle of the stage, a black-haired boy appears out of thin air. His hair is long but scraped into a pony tail. He's wearing a cream-patterned shirt with a tongue-shaped collar and matching trousers that flare out a little at the bottom. The pattern has the outline of blue flowers that look like someone doodled them onto an exercise pad. I used to doodle all the time when I was in Sixth Year. I was almost excluded for excessive doodling.

This is the best doodling flower pattern I've ever seen. Is it some futuristic fashion? Whatever it is, I love it. He's carrying a cream-coloured suitcase with more lines on it than Millennia's face. The boy looks about 15 and is as beautiful as a girl.

Millennia looks cross. The lines on her face etch deeper. Her cat's eyes narrow.

'GMT. So glad you chose to finally join us.'

And then I realise that if this is GMT then he must be a she because she's sharing our chalet. I didn't recognise her because in the film her hair was straggly like Millennia's, not tied back. Millennia seems to increase in size and her voice goes up in volume, like a Head Teacher on a loudspeaker.

'You're late!'

'I leaped from '68. Think you'd call that early, man.'

Some of the pupils laugh but I don't because one; it isn't true, GMT IS late and two; she spoke back to an elder and tried to humiliate them and three; she has an American accent and I want to know if she's from New York because Bob Beamon was from New York, so she might have met him in 1968.

Millennia pauses for a very long time but says nothing at all until GMT looks from side to side, picks up her suitcase, walks down the steps on the left side of the stage then stands against the long white wall. She looks back up at the stage and winks. MC^2 winks back. I went through a winking stage. I used to practise in front of the mirror. First it was hard. Then I got quite good. Then I stopped doing it in case I did it by mistake and people would stare at me.

I almost do it by mistake now. Maybe it's contagious. I'm

scrunching up my left eye when my right one notices GMT's wearing two watches, one on each wrist. I can't see the details but one has a blue leather strap and the other looks shiny and metallic. I'll ask her about the two watches later.

Millennia presses a button and 'Useful Information' flashes on the screen behind her. She talks us through it and I read it on the screen at the same time to remember it better.

'You have met the subject leaders. They are specialists in their field. Le Temps, in particular, has transformed these grounds from a country park to an eco-paradise.' She smiles at Le Temps from East to West then shakes her head like it's full of buzzing flies. 'We value their human input, their uniqueness. For that reason, this is a robot-free zone.'

Some of the children boo. I'm a bit sad because I was looking forward to seeing the eco-robots collect rubbish and do other jobs humans don't want to do. Millennia waits for silence.

'Each leader is known by their initial:

I, Millennia, am known as Miss M;

Season is Mrs S;

Le Temps equals Mr T.'

When she says his name, she sounds French and smiles at him again. I think Millennia might be in love with Le Temps. Maybe he's her husband. But she's 200 years old and he's about 40, so that would be a very strange match, even in 2048 when age doesn't matter.

Millennia continues:

'MC^2 = Mr E. He will explain why later. Our offices are all on the lower ground floor if you need us. The Time-Outer-

Space and SENsory Room are also on the lower ground floor.'

I read about that in the itinerary. In the future, all new buildings have to provide a room for people with specialist needs like me.

Millennia pauses to allow us to take in all this information. Some of us are reading and watching it on the screen but a few are listening with their eyes closed like it's so boring they've fallen asleep. Then Millennia's voice changes. She sounds like Millennia through a crackly loudspeaker. I don't like Millennia. She keeps changing. One minute she speaks slowly and clearly, the next minute she's too loud.

'There is something I must disclose to you all: there have been a few disappearances on previous leap weeks. Some Leaplings misuse their freedom, abuse their Gift. They leap and refuse to come back. We have spent days, weeks, months of valuable time attempting to locate them.

'Due to the misdemeanours of that tiny minority, we have cancelled the trip to London this Tuesday.'

Lots of boos until the teachers calm us down. We were all looking forward to seeing London almost drowned after the rise in sea levels. Millennia continues to talk over us.

'Some of us will spend the day on Missing Leapling Alert. My colleagues Mrs S and Mr T will manage the centre.

'Bissextiles take heed: it is an immense privilege to be chosen for Leap 2048. I trust you will honour the PRESENT and have no ambitions for the past, or the future.' When she says the word 'past' she gives me the cat's eye for three long seconds. That's odd. Why does Millennia hate me when she's never met me before? Do I look like a missing Leapling?

Millennia sits down. Some of the teachers pull their eyebrows down to their eyes and tap into their phones, some begin to clap, the children who had their eyes closed have what-big-eyes to the power of 3. Which Leapling would dare leap away from a school trip? You'd have to be REALLY bad to do something like that. Everyone's talking at once except Ama. She's shaking her head from side to side. Her lips are pursed shut and her cheeks are wet.

∞

They tell us which groups we'll be in, one for workshops, the other for chalets where we sleep. The chalets are called The Hives. I remember seeing them in the video. I can't wait to see what they look like inside.

My workshop group is: me, Big Ben, Ama and GMT.

My chalet group is all girls: me, Ama, Noon and GMT. Three palindromes out of four!

Le Temps leads our workshop group. He also looks bigger than in the video. Maybe they used a camera that zoomed out instead of in. Le Temps is a big, bald man who looks like he goes to the gym, even though he's old.

'So, Leapers,' he says in his buttery voice, 'I'd like you each to introduce yourself by name and say a little bit about its origins. All your names are special. GMT, begin please.'

'I'm GMT,' she says. 'I named myself for Greenwich Mean Time, man, the world standard for clocks.'

'Really?' says Le Temps, rolling his eyes clockwise. 'I thought it stood for Genetically Modified Teen.'

GMT narrows her eyes at Le Temps. It wasn't a very good joke. I learnt about Greenwich Mean Time in PPF. It's the normal time in the UK in the winter and spring. Then the government make the clocks go forward for an hour in British Summertime, which messes up my head. All other countries are either hours ahead (+) or hours behind (-) Greenwich Mean Time. Mexico City is six hours behind GMT. It's a great name for a Leapling.

'That's why you wear two watches?' Ama says.

'Yeah, kinda. One for GMT,' she holds up her left wrist with the blue leather strap, 'and the other for whenever I'm at.'

I stare at the chunky metallic watch on her right wrist. It looks like something that hasn't been invented yet. She sees me looking.

'Solar-powered,' she says. 'In summertime. But when I'm looping, I batterise. Keeps track of the years.'

I have no idea what she's talking about. Le Temps intervenes.

'Looping is when you leap and stay there for some months or years. Loopers often have a favourite year they like to live in. They wear two watches, to keep track of the new time and the old. Ama, could you introduce yourself?'

'Ama Atta Asante. Ama means born on Saturday in Akan. That's Ghanaian. Everyone's named after days of the week. Mum's from Ghana, Dad's from here. None of us Leaplings,' she shrugs, 'except my brother.'

Ama looks at her feet. Le Temps frowns.

'Why did you come here, Ama?'

Silence. Why shouldn't Ama come here? What an odd question. I find myself speaking before thinking.

'Ama had to come to be my mentor because 2048 is her present but my future and I might find it difficult.'

Ama looks up at me and smiles slightly before looking at her feet again. Le Temps says nothing. I look across the room at the other two groups. I can hear everything they're saying. Season's group are laughing about Martin Aston's name. In MC²'s group, Maria's explaining how her parents didn't want relatives in Brazil to know her birth date in case she had The Gift and they found out, so they gave her a normal name but when she grows up she plans to change it. I hear both groups simultaneously until it starts to sound like German and I have to really focus to bring my mind back to our group. Then I feel a knot in my stomach when Le Temps turns to me. But I've been rehearsing whilst the others were speaking. I take a deep breath.

'I'm Elle Bíbi-Imbelé Ifíè. Elle is a palindrome, which means it reads the same backwards or forwards, and it means she in French. Bíbi-Imbelé means mouth-sweet in Izon, which is a language from Nigeria. Ifíè means time.'

'Thank you, Elle,' says Le Temps. 'That was quite a monologue in your mouth-sweet tongue. But,' he takes his Chronophone out of his pocket and taps it on, 'can you actually SPEAK Izon?'

I look down at my shoes. Grandma chose not to speak to me in Izon when I was little because I didn't speak at all till my first leap birthday. She was worried if she spoke Izon to me I would get confused and speak a weird mixture of English and Izon called Englon or Izlish. I liked the idea. But I didn't speak at all for years. I had to go to Speech and Language classes where they threw a red ball at me and made me throw it back. Grandma stopped me going because she wanted me to learn to speak English, not play ball games. That was the day she said, 'If your tongue refuses to speak, I will teach it to dance.' She meant I would learn how to taste things. She taught me to cook.

Le Temps looks up from his phone. 'Thought not,' he says. 'Maybe one day you'll learn to live up to your name, eh?'

He smiles like he just said something nice but he didn't. He puts his phone away.

'And last but by no means least, Ben.'

After a six-second delay, Big Ben says, 'Yes.'

'Introduce yourself.' Le Temps is staring at Big Ben.

Big Ben is staring at Le Temps. 'Ben,' he says.

Le Temps shakes his head and wrinkles his forehead till it looks like sand ripples on the beach. He's still staring at Big Ben. I want Big Ben to say something about being nicknamed Big Ben because he's big and broad and he likes keeping time like the bell in the Houses of Parliament, but he doesn't say anything. That means he doesn't like Le Temps. Big Ben's very good at judging character.

Le Temps stops staring and smiles at us all.

'As you all know, I'm Le Temps. Le Temps means weather in French.'

I knew that but Big Ben wouldn't have known. Le Temps almost whispers the next sentence, so we have to really concentrate.

'Le Temps also means time. In the abstract.'

Our mouths move like we're saying WOW but me most of all. That's the best name ever! I have no idea what 'in the abstract' means but I'll look it up. Imagine having a name that means two different things at the same time! I wish we didn't have to call him Mr T. I decide to call him Mr T to his face but Le Temps in my head.

'Are you French?'

The words come out before I can stop them. I wanted to say a longer sentence because in school they tell us we have to ask questions and give answers in full sentences and this is a bit like school. I hope I don't get into trouble. Le Temps smiles like his teeth are stuck together.

'No. English as they come. But French is the best language.'

After that, Le Temps asks us what we want to achieve this week. GMT wants to learn more about the eco-ethics of the centre, man. Ama wants to learn mentoring so she can run activity camps when she's a grown-up. I say I want to become more confident because the future is better for Leaplings like me. But that isn't primarily what I want. What I really really want is to know what SOS L means. But I can't say that because no one knows about the Predictive. It isn't lying. It's just saying ONE of the things I want to achieve this week. Big Ben doesn't say anything. I don't think he likes Le Temps because he doesn't drive a Ferrari or rap.

Next, we're given our Chronophones. Le Temps says he's happy to look after our normal phones but I don't hand mine in because I don't know Le Temps and I don't like other people touching my phone, except Big Ben, who uses it to time my runs. My Chronophone is black and larger than I expected. Maybe they have to be big to send messages to the past, present and future. Or so people don't lose them. When technology gets sophisticated, they make everything too small and it's counter-productive. Grandma's always losing her phone.

I barely look at it before I put it in my bag. Big Ben seems quite excited about his and starts researching Futuristic Ferraris and how they operate. Ama's excited too, until GMT explains Annuals need extra training to send messages across time, though they can send across space. Then Ama looks sad again, which makes me feel sad. I decide I like Ama even though I hardly know her. Even if she turns out to hate athletics. She has an even better name than Noon.

But the best name of all, even better than Ama, is Le Temps. When I hear it in my head, it's Millennia's voice sounding French; when I SEE it, it's capital letters flying all over a screen like flies, till they form words, a caption:

LE TEMPS.

∞ Chapter 08:00 ∞

UNDERCOVER

The Hives are modelled on beehives! They look like upside-down straw baskets made of wood. I'm staying in Hive 1. You go through the door and there's a round lounge with lots of yellow beanbags at the edges and a hexagonal rug in the middle that's woven from straw. The windows are hexagons too! Then you go up wooden stairs that curve around the outside wall to the bedroom, which has two sets of bunk beds and fitted wardrobes and another rug. The perfect treehouse for human bees!

We've come back to our chalets to unpack. Le Temps had to help me with my suitcase. He complained it wasn't on wheels but the only ones on wheels were black and I wanted a white one.

'What are you carrying in there, Elle, dead bodies?'

'No. Yams,' I said.

I don't know why he was smiling. It wasn't a very good joke.

Ama and I are here first, as the others had to register. Mrs C Eckler has come across to help me get unpacked. I get upset when she opens my suitcase. There's a blanket I don't recognise and some white bras.

'They're not my clothes.'

Mrs C Eckler pulls out a white cotton jumper a few layers down. 'This is definitely yours, I've seen you wearing it.'

Then I realise Grandma must have packed some extra things. Grandma is obsessed with bras. Bras are her specialist subject. She kept shouting from the bedroom, 'Elle, remember to pack your brassiere. No wibble-wobble!' She knows I hate wearing bras. I can't breathe in them.

Mrs C Eckler takes my yams to be stored in the pantry, then leaves. They've labelled our beds. I'm on the bottom bunk and GMT is on the top. Ama's on the bottom of the other bunk and Noon is on the top. The rules say the older ones take the top bunk so there's no arguing. Ama stares out of the window for a second.

'Elle, thanks for covering for me earlier.'

I shrug my shoulders. 'He asked why you came here and you went tongue-tied. Why did you come here?'

'Can you keep a secret?'

I nod. I'm very good with secrets but you have to be careful. Some secrets can get you into trouble.

'What kind of secret?' I say.

She turns to face me, but her eyes are looking elsewhere. She's looking up at the ceiling above her bunk bed. 'Oh my God!'

I look where she's looking. A huge brown spider stares back at us. It's so big I can see its multiple eyes. Its legs are as thick as my fingers, but it's a mutant. It only has six legs, like a daddy-long-legs. I hope it can't fly. They warned us spiders are bigger in the future because of global warming. More insects for them to eat. It should be in a zoo, not in our chalet.

'Wow!' I say.

'Get a teacher!' Ama doesn't like spiders. But I don't mind them. I climb up the steps onto Noon's bed and very very slowly reach out my hand and Ama screams and it scuttles away across the ceiling. She scared it away, not me.

'Don't worry,' I say. 'It's only a spider. I need a cup.'

'I'll check the bathroom.'

The bathrooms are underground. I haven't been down there yet, but I saw the stairs spiralling down from the lounge. The spider's moved across the ceiling above the other bunk beds. I'm quicker this time. I reach out my hand and grab one of its legs. The spider scrunches itself up, playing dead. I open the window and it scuttles down the wall.

I join Ama in the bathroom.

'Check out the showers.'

They're motion-operated. You flutter your fingers to make them come on and push your hand up to make them stop, push your hands out to make them hotter and pull your hands in to make them colder. The lights are motion-operated too. And you can programme the walls so they look like a tropical rainforest or a scene with blue sky, green fields and mountains. It will take some getting used to. But Ama lives in 2048. It's normal for her.

She's still thinking about the spider, even though it's gone away.

'You were so brave, Elle.'

'I'm only scared of things I can't see.'

Like whether I'm going to be bullied or excluded. And Grandma not being able to get back up the stairs. And SOS L. Things are always worse when you can't see them, when they MIGHT happen and you don't know HOW they'll happen and your mind thinks of a thousand horrible things that COULD happen. When they happen, I'm not scared any more.

We go back up to the lounge because the showers make me feel claustrophobic. I don't like not having any windows, even though it's clever to build showers underground that look like you're outdoors and they're very eco-friendly. Then I remember Ama wanted to tell me a secret. She looks out of the windows like she's scared the spider will come back.

'Elle. You won't tell anyone, will you?' She lowers her voice to a whisper. 'I'm here undercover.'

There's silence in the room. Then I speak.

'Are you a police officer?'

'No, of course not. I'm only 14. No . . .' She looks serious again. 'I'm not here to make friends, I'm here to find my—'

GMT bursts through the door with her battered cream suitcase. Noon follows silently behind. Ama smiles at them.

'You took your time. These chalets are wreckage!' and she's bounding up the stairs and we follow and she's throwing clothes out of her suitcase onto her bed, leaving me standing in the middle of the room thinking if I don't find out what she was going to say, I'll die. If she doesn't tell me soon, I'll spend the whole day guessing what she was going to say until I get a headache or have to do running round the track or the woods or whatever.

Luckily, I happen to look down at the floor and see Noon's beautiful pair of two-tone leather shoes and decide to talk to her instead.

I say, 'Where did you buy your shoes?'

and she says, 'Do you have a gramophone for the Charleston?'

at exactly the same time.

I don't know what a gramophone is, or the Charleston, and I'm scared to repeat my question in case it comes out wrong, so I turn away from her to GMT, who's sorting clothes onto hangers and in drawers. I sit cross-legged in the middle of the rug.

'Are your clothes from the future?'

'No, honeybee, they're '68 head to toe. Don't mix my years.'

'What do you mean? Do you only wear clothes from 1968?'

'Sure,' she says in her American accent.

'Are you autistic?'

'In the here and now, I might be diagnosed. Back in '68 they thought only boys with speech delay had it. But my parents were cool, they taught me to vibe off my strengths.'

She's hanging some outfits in the wardrobe and they all have patterns on them or are made of suede, which is the opposite side of leather, in lime-green and mango.

'Are you from New York City? Have you met Bob Beamon?'

'No to both. Who's Bob Beamon?'

She hasn't heard of Bob Beamon! I can't believe she's never heard of the greatest long jumper of all time! But I carry on. 'Are you from Boston, Massachusetts?'

I know Boston, Massachusetts is in America and I want to go there because it's the best place name ever, all those sibilants. Sibilants are when you repeat the letter S. Mississippi is the name of a river and a state in America which has four Ss too and is my second favourite. Missouri is my third.

'No, I'm from everyplace. But I've looped California, West Coast,' she says, hanging up strings of beads on the dressing-table mirror, ''67 to '68. Then back to Britain till '71' – she takes out the hair tie, shakes out her wild, black hair. Now she looks like the girl in the photo – 'when they went decimal and put the clocks back again.'

I read somewhere that people went crazy in 1971 because they got used to the clocks not changing for three years then the government made them go back again, plus they changed all the money so people didn't know how to buy a loaf of bread. 1971 sounds like hell. No wonder GMT went back to 1968.

'Are you from Britain or America?'

'Both. Born in Britain 2004, bred late '60s, West Coast, United States. Flower Power loopers. Kinda raised myself.'

'Didn't you have any parents?'

'They leaped all over the timeline so I didn't see them much. Papa's Annual, so he held tight onto Mama's hand. She sure can leap!' She pulls out a crumpled black-and-white photo of a man and woman with black hair and olive skin who look like twins. 'That's them. Free spirits both. Native blood.'

'Why do you look like a boy?'

'A boy?' She smiles. 'Thought I was more, kinda, androgynous. Look like a girl AND a boy. Anyway, easier to look like a boy when you loop the past. Less hassle.'

'Are you a bisexual bissextile?' I've always wanted to say that.

She throws back her head and laughs out loud this time. 'Guess you'd call me that in '68. But now . . .' She looks out of the window as if the word is hidden somewhere in the woods. 'Who knows? They don't care WHO you love, long as you love Planet Earth.'

She didn't answer my question properly, but at least I know she's a girl. If she was a boy, she shouldn't be sharing our chalet. It would be breaking the rules. If I was a boy, I wouldn't be called Elle. I'd be called Il and it wouldn't be a palindrome.

I sit down at the mirror and start taking out my cornrow. It still hurts and I don't like looking different in the mirror. And I love combing my hair, its frizz, the fuzziness of it in my hands, the smell of the pomade when I rub it down the parting into my scalp. I'm using my white afro comb, combing my hair out to a halo almost as big as Ama's.

There's strange music playing in the background. While I was talking to GMT, Ama was talking to Noon. Music was coming from Noon's phone and she was doing this strange dance in the middle of the room with her arms and legs flapping so she looked like Big Ben when he's excited. I've never seen anything like it! Ama started copying the moves till she was in synch with Noon. Then I saw why Ama goes to Triple M School. She's a brilliant dancer. Noon was dancing so hard she almost trod on me. She looked happy for the first time. She must be very brave leaping all on her own from 1924. Also, she's clever because she learnt to use the Chronophone in five minutes and in the 1920s they didn't even have mobiles. I part my hair down the middle and comb each side into a bunch. I take the white bobbles out of my pocket and secure the bunches. Now I look like me.

I look across the room at Ama. She's still chatting to Noon, who's sitting on the top bunk where the spider was living. Noon doesn't speak much but Ama fills in the gaps. I wonder whether Ama wants to be my friend or does she prefer Noon now because Noon doesn't speak as much as I do. I feel sad when I think that. I wonder what Ama's really thinking. Ama is a secret agent. She hasn't told me her secret yet. Maybe I'll stay up all night wondering what her secret is. She said, 'I'm here to find my—'

What has she lost? What is she looking for?

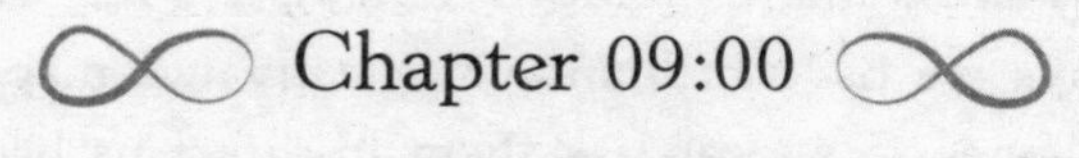

Chapter 09:00
CAKE

I don't have a chance to speak to Ama again before lunch, when they announce an Oops. Due to the heavy rain, they've postponed the tour of the grounds till tomorrow. Our cookery session with Season will take place instead. I like cooking but I find it difficult to edit the changed timetable in my head. Mrs C Eckler has to sit with me at the end of lunch because I haven't eaten my potato soup. It feels like my voice is stuck halfway down my throat.

'Elle,' she says, 'how about a walk outside? Season won't mind if we're a bit late back.'

I nod. I think I need to do some running. Big Ben is running up and down the café. I think he could do with some running too. As if Mrs C Eckler reads my mind, she calls Big Ben over and we put our waterproofs on.

∞

It's raining cows and bulls, hurting my face as it turns to hailstones the size of golf balls. But it's still mild. Big Ben and I start running as soon as we get outside and Mrs C Eckler's finding it difficult to keep up with us. There are lots of woodland paths and we have no idea where we're going but Mrs C Eckler says we have brilliant voice-activated maps on our Chronophones so we can ask them to direct us back to the centre. We MUST stay together and keep our phones on so she can track us.

'I know I can trust you both.'

'What do you mean?' I say.

'Not to get lost. Or . . . leap somewhere else.' Mrs C Eckler looks like she's aged ten years since this morning.

'We wouldn't do that. We're running.'

I look at Mrs C Eckler. Does she know I did a solo leap on Wednesday?

Big Ben and I accelerate into the woods. The hail is falling through the leaves like an orchestra. Everything's green and shiny. I love it here.

'Am I your boyfriend?' says Big Ben, jogging beside me on his tiptoes.

'No,' I say.

'Can I time you?'

'OK.'

I'm not wearing the right trainers, but it feels good to be in the fresh air. There are lots of trees which shield us from the golf balls. It's always easy to talk to Big Ben because he doesn't make fun of me. I have to explain things to him sometimes, and sometimes he takes a long time to answer, but he likes running and he doesn't tell me I speak like a robot.

There are lots of mushrooms under the trees, all different kinds in clusters like flowers. Mushrooms look beautiful but most of them are poisonous and can kill you. The brightest-coloured ones are toadstools, mostly red and yellow. Some look like ears that have been twisted and stretched. Some look like the ones that grow out of the wall in our lounge. They make me think about Grandma. I hope she's all right on her own.

Big Ben starts making humming noises, pretending to be a Ferrari. He accelerates up a side-path so fast I have trouble keeping up with him, even though I'm almost 90% age grade on the junior Parkrun. I'm tall but nowhere near as tall as Big Ben. He's 5 foot 11 and still growing!

There are slippery steps which go on forever. I notice large clusters of bluebells each side. They're a deep shade of lilac and smell heavenly. At the top, a field with a few cows. I forgot there might be animals. I thought they didn't farm animals in 2048 because it was against the law as they make too much poo which makes global warming. There are only ten cows in the whole field. I came here on a school trip in Sixth Year when it was a country park and we saw some ponies. I don't think it belongs to the council any more. Maybe it belongs to the Time Squad.

We run along the right side of the field and follow the path all the way round. It's stopped hailing now and is only lightly raining. The birds are singing, as if to say thank goodness the hail has stopped. It's lighter up here and the sun's trying to come out. I wish for a double rainbow. I love rainbows. I'm just getting into my stride now Big Ben's slowed down, getting into the zone.

I'm in the zone when I see the hat.

I think it's a toadstool at first, because it's bright red and covered in mud and set back in some trees. But it's not the right shape to be a toadstool.

'Big Ben,' I say, and he slows down beside me. 'Look!'

I don't know why I've stopped. It's only a hat and I don't need a hat. I have my own white one and I'd never wear a red hat. And it's covered in mud. It's not like a February day in 2020 at all. It's like April, mild and raining all the time. Not hat weather. You can smell the bluebells, even in the rain.

Big Ben picks it up and puts it on his head. I can't believe he did that.

'You'll get a disease and die,' I say.

He just runs off. And I want to be in the zone again, so I run off too. We go all the way round the outside of the field. The cows ignore us.

Even though I'm sweaty from running, and in the zone, the rain's so heavy it's going through my clothes. I want to keep running because it feels good, but there are too many puddles to jump over. Even Bob Beamon wouldn't want to jump over that many puddles. I tell Big Ben I want to go back. He turns round immediately. I always decide how long or far we're going to run and he never argues. He's still wearing the hat covered in mud and twigs. It makes him look like he has mini antlers, like a man-beast hybrid. I don't tell him, though.

Mrs C Eckler is still standing outside, totally soaked. When she sees us, she puts her phone away. I think she likes the rain. Why else would she stand outside so long?

∞

We're in The Beanstalk kitchen. Like the café, there's lots of light. It's a large square, with white ovens all down one side. In the middle is a huge, square worktop covered with mixing bowls and ingredients. Season is making a birthday cake for the Leap Party. We're making cupcakes that will decorate the main cake. The main cake will be made up of four cakes: a two, a zero, a four and an eight. As so many of us have a birthday today, they can't put the right number of candles on, so it's better to celebrate the year.

We help Season put coconut cream and white sugar in a bowl, then sift in white flour and lots of baking powder to make it rise. The baking powder is instead of eggs. The cake is totally vegan and made of all white ingredients! I've never heard of a cake like that before. We all have a go at making the cake because Season says food made with love tastes better. Season tells us what to do but sometimes forgets the right words and we help her fill them in. She says it's her age. She does lots of meaningful pausing when she speaks. And she gets power surges. Her body gets so hot she can burn toast.

'It'll be brown on top when it's cooked,' Season explains as she puts the cake in the oven, 'and a creamy colour inside, but we're going to cover it in white icing.' She smiles at me. 'I hope you'll have a slice when it's finished!'

'Maybe,' I say. Maybe it would be OK to eat a different colour food here. It's so different here in 2048 – not being bullied by Pete LMS, my words coming out the RIGHT way. It's nice being with the 2048 pupils too. Ama's telling me all about her school.

'We don't have bullying,' she says, 'because everyone knows the cameras record it as evidence.'

'Don't the bullies steal your phone?'

'Nah.' She shakes her head. 'Overhead cameras. Concealed, like CCTV. They know they're being filmed, so they don't try.'

'Why didn't any of your Leaplings come on this trip?'

'They leapt to 2096! I don't know where they went. Not here.' She smiles, showing her gap. 'You've got flour all over your face.'

It must have been when I opened the packet. It came out in a cloud.

'Are you a Vegan?'

'No.' She laughs and lowers her voice. 'I eat meat on a Sunday, so I can't call myself Vegan. My parents don't believe in Veganism.'

'You make it sound like a religion?'

'It is for some. Strict Hindus don't eat meat. We're Christians. Kind of.' She raises one eyebrow; I don't know how she does it. 'You?'

'Grandma's Christian to the power of 3!' I brush the flour off my face and sneeze. 'If you're not a Vegan, what are you? A Vegetable or a Meathead?'

Ama laughs. 'You know about the Meat Wars? Not everyone falls into those two camps. We're Omnivores, aka Omni, I suppose. We eat meat but keep to the rations. Mum's worried it's all GM. Used to eat fish on Fridays but fish are retro.'

'We learnt that in PPF.' I stir the flour into the mixture. It looks like it's curdled so I use the whisk. I learnt THAT in cookery. But I don't want to think about school.

'Yeh. They rationed it cos no one listened. You get the eco-warrior types, the Vegetables, some of them Vegan,' she nods towards Season, 'and the Meatheads who have to eat meat every day or they'll die. In the end, there were so many Meatheads there wasn't enough land to grow anything else. Food chain slumped. Scientists started growing meat in labs.'

'So they don't do intensive dairy farming any more?' I read about intensive farming for my geography project.

'You totally get it,' Ama said. 'Shall we cook these cakes, then?'

'Am I your boyfriend?'

Big Ben joins us. I don't know where he's been up till now. He's soaked through, so maybe he just stood outside for an hour. He's taken the hat off, though. He wanders to the other side of the kitchen and looks out the window. I realise he's gazing at Fiona the Ferrari.

'ARE you his girlfriend?' Ama says. 'Think he likes you.'

'Me? No. Big Ben just likes timing me run,' I say. 'Fiona's his girlfriend.'

The smell of the main cake cooking is making me hungry. I hardly ate any lunch and running always makes me hungry. I scrape the spoon round the inside of the bowl and taste it. Not bad. Maybe I'll try a slice of birthday cake later. If I could last that long before dying of hunger. The others are tasting the mixture too. I worry we'll eat it all before the cake goes into the oven. Then we'll all starve this evening.

'Something smells good.' Le Temps strides into the room in green wellington boots, leaving footprints all over the white floor. 'Let me guess, birthday cake?'

Season looks at the footprints and her eyebrows drop down to her eyes. He disappears into a side door and appears a minute later carrying a clear bag containing what is obviously large chunks of meat. Season goes white and her voice sounds distorted, like she's virtually tongue-tied, struggling to get each word out.

'Mr T. What, exactly, are you doing carrying meat, in a meat-free zone?'

'Carrying meat in a meat-free zone.' He grins.

'On whose authority?'

'Infinity's,' he says, no longer grinning, and Season jumps a little at the name. 'Meat's permissible on leap birthdays. Special occasion, remember? Some of us CAN taste the difference between animal and vegetable. It's Armageddon outside. Where else could I preserve it? Sorry, old bean.'

And off he walks into the grounds. We all look at each other. I'm the first to speak.

'Who's Infinity?'

Ama makes what-big-eyes. 'You never heard of Infinity? She's the wisest bissextile of all but no one's ever seen her.'

'Like a god?'

'No. More like an elder everyone respects.'

'Can she live forever?'

'No one can. But rumour has it she can leap to the far edges of time.'

I want to ask more questions but Season's throwing washing-up into the sink. I'm worried the cakes are going to burn because she might have a mega power surge and burn them and we won't be able to have our party. As I think that, the buzzer goes off to say the cakes are ready and Season puts on the oven gloves and asks for two volunteers to get the cake racks out. Big Ben and Noon put their hands up. I notice Noon's wearing a pair of jeans which she must have borrowed from Ama because she wouldn't have jeans in 1924. Maybe Ama would rather be friends with Noon than with me. I'm sad when I think that.

But I don't think that for long because I'm thinking about Infinity, the person and the symbol ∞. Infinity is the wisest bissextile of them all. And MC^2 has an infinity tattoo on his left hand . . .

Chapter 10:00

GAME

We open our birthday presents at 6 p.m. in the Common Room. I've never been in there before. There are lots of comfy chocolate-brown chairs and circular rugs with jagged patterns on them in cream, black and gold. I get a book about Bob Beamon. His wife helped him write it. Maybe he's like Big Ben and needs help with typing. I can't wait to read it. It's not really a children's book. In the future, they don't believe in separating the two. They think children shouldn't be sheltered from bad things. GMT gets a new watch. Maybe it's one MC^2 stole from another century. Those two have definitely met before. Big Ben gets a stopwatch that can time nanoseconds. I've never heard him whoop so loud. Ama doesn't get anything because she's an Annual.

We're having a barbecue outside instead of the usual evening meal in The Beanstalk. The air's mild and damp and there's music to help us relax but it's a bit loud. There are two separate grills, meat and vegetarian. Le Temps is in charge of the meat, which is why he collected it earlier and made Season cross. And you'll never guess who's slapping meat on the barbecue. An eco-bot! The bot looks like someone squashed together old clothes, metal cans and cardboard boxes to make something that LOOKS like a human. Their face is patchworked, and they're wearing a black beanie. Some of the boys are pointing and laughing.

GMT's staring at the eco-bot. She's wearing a long purple velvet gown, long black beads and has her hair parted in the middle and hanging loose. It's quite hard to see her eyes and she keeps pushing the hair out of her face. I like the gown, though. I think she's having trouble looking at the eco-bot because she has too much hair, but then she says:

'Holy Joe, it's them!'

'Who?' I say.

'Mange-Tout. Why're they here?

'Who is THEY?'

'Neither he nor she. Mange-Tout. Eco-bot 350. Lives off waste and recycles ideas.'

I frown like Grandma at the Eco-bot 350. 'They shouldn't be here. This is a robot-free zone.'

GMT's still staring. 'Used to be big on the Veggie scene but they switched.'

'What's that in English?' says Ama.

Ama's wearing a shiny orange bomber jacket the same colour as her hair and silver trousers that have a skirt on top in the same material. I blink. When I look again, the jacket has turned turquoise! Noon's standing behind her, wearing a pale yellow dress almost down to her ankles covered in cream beads. It's so sparkly, I can only look at it if I squint my eyes and look sideways. It's beautiful, though. GMT lowers her voice.

'Mange-Tout was eco-royalty for a decade. Vegetable veteran. A soundbite for animal rights. Most Veggies were eco-only but Mange-Tout was retro. Said animals had the same rights as people. Their slogan was MAN=BEAST. Bot was cool, man.' She shakes her head and her hair goes into her eyes again. 'Then they malfunctioned. Went mute. No one knows why.'

Ama nods. 'Think I heard something,' she says. 'Didn't they make a public—?'

'Yeah. "I EAT MY WORDS. EAT EVERYTHING." Then disappeared. There were rumours. And now they're here.'

I stare over at the barbecue. Mange-Tout stares back and bares their teeth like a smile. But their teeth are metal. They don't look happy, they look angry, like a mad metallic dog. They look like they don't know what a vegetable is. They must have been totally reprogrammed. I turn my head but still watch them out of the corner of my eye as they slap more meat on the barbecue and say something to Le Temps. But GMT says they went mute. Obviously they are talking again now. I wonder if Mange-Tout sounds like a person or a machine. By now, most of the group are staring with eyes big as Mars. GMT takes one last look at Mange-Tout and the meat barbecue then walks over to the veggie one and we slowly follow.

Season has made lots of vegetarian options, some 'Real', like vegetable kebabs, which are different vegetables on sticks. She colour-coded them so one has things like yellow peppers, yellow courgettes, sweetcorn and golden tofu; one has aubergine, red onions and red peppers; and one has a lumpy green vegetable I don't recognise and green peppers. And some 'Substitutes', like beancon and soysages. Season says it's better to eat 'Real' food, but if you like meat you should eat the substitutes. There are all kinds of colourful dips set up to look like a painter's palette in small, circular bowls. There's a sign over the dips saying *Pique Your Palate*, which means taste. I like the homophones 'palette' and 'palate'.

I'm enjoying being outside, even though it's noisy with people talking over the music. This track's a weird instrumental from 2048. It has fast drums like a heartbeat, frogs croaking and birdsong. The 2048 pupils are swaying to it, nodding their heads, and Ama's twitching her body like a sparrow on a bird-bath. Her jacket's gone glossy black. She doesn't look human! Then I realise they must be playing music from different leap years. When I first came outside, they were playing a song called 'Crosstown Traffic' by Jimi Hendrix, which came out in 1968. He was a black rock star from America, so maybe he knew Bob Beamon.

On the side of the main building is a large canopy so all the food and people can stay dry. It's still murgy after the storm. Murgy is a mixture of muggy and murky.

I love the smell of the food on the barbecues, even though everything smells a bit burnt. I hope Mange-Tout and Season don't completely burn the food. Further away from the building is a small fire where one of the Triple M teachers is cooking jacket potatoes. I decide that's what I'm going to eat, with one of Season's white dips, followed by birthday cake.

All the pupils and tutors are here. Everyone has dressed up because it's a VERY SPECIAL OCCASION, even people who hate clothes. I'm wearing a white jumpsuit that glows in the dark. I packed it specially because we were going to the future and it looked like a spacesuit. It's also waterproof so very practical for damp future weather. Even Big Ben is dressed up. He's wearing some black skinny jeans that make his legs look even longer than they are, a red jumper and, would you believe, the red hat we found in the undergrowth! He hasn't even bothered to take out the twigs and it still has mud on it. Classic Big Ben!

Mrs C Eckler is wearing a sparkly silver top and black shiny trousers. I love her top. I keep squinting my eyes so the sparkles dance in the light. Her hair is piled up on her head, with a sunflower pinned on the left-hand side. Her husband is also wearing black shiny trousers but his top is plain grey. She's eating some of the red vegetable kebabs.

'Can I get you something, Elle?'

'I'm waiting for the potatoes.'

The barbecues are making me hungry though, Mange-Tout cooking on one and Season on the other. A stereo of smells. Ama says they do that to keep the meat separate from the vegetables. I like that because I like to keep food separate on my plate, even though it's the same colour. If it mixes, there are too many textures to cope with and I don't enjoy the food. I wander over to the meat barbecue expecting to see burgers and sausages but that isn't what's there. It looks like steaks. The Leaplings gather around the meat table because we aren't used to so many vegetables. I think most of the 2048 pupils are Vegan except Ama.

'There's nothing better than the smell of meat on a barbecue,' says Le Temps. 'Actually, there is. Eating it.'

'Is it ready yet?' says Jake.

'Indeed,' says Le Temps, putting the steaks onto white bread rolls. 'And now, the moment of truth. If anyone can tell me what kind of meat it is, you get to drive Season's Ferrari.' He pauses. 'Only joking.'

It isn't a very good joke. But Big Ben grabs a roll on the word 'Ferrari'. He wants to drive. I hope he manages to guess correctly. He takes a huge bite and immediately opens his mouth like he wants to spit it out.

'Is it disgusting?'

Big Ben does his three-second pause and mutters something that sounds like too hot. Of course it was too hot. It came off the barbecue 20 seconds ago! Then his voice sounds normal again.

'Is it cows?'

He's thinking about the cows we saw in the field earlier. It isn't a bad guess. If they live on this land, maybe they kill one every four years for the Leap Party barbecue.

Le Temps shakes his head. 'Try again.'

Big Ben chews for a few seconds. 'Pork chop.'

'No.' Le Temps smiles. 'Here's a clue: something you might come across in the grounds here. If you look far enough ahead.'

'Rabbit,' says Jake.

'Fox,' says Maria.

They're both wrong. It's far too big to be rabbit. And you can't eat foxes. Everyone knows that.

'Is it goat?' I say. At that moment they start to play some of that 1924 music Noon likes and she and Ama go crazy dancing, all arms and legs.

'Not a bad guess for someone who only eats yams. But wrong.'

'What is it then?'

'Now that would be telling. It would spoil the game. The game is to guess.'

I look at Big Ben. He's screwing up his face to think.

'Deer? Badgers? Monkeys?' he says.

Le Temps looks angry and scared. I wonder if he gets a headache when he feels like that. He talks to Big Ben's hat, not his face.

'SENSIBLE guesses. Since when did monkeys live in the woods?'

'We only saw cows,' says Big Ben.

'So you met my prize herd in the woods today? Who gave you permission to go there?'

'Mrs C Eckler,' I say.

'Looks like you brought the woods back with you.'

He's looking at Big Ben's hat, with the dirt and twigs in it. Big Ben looks back at him.

'Lamb?'

'No.'

'Sheep, then. It must be sheep, by process of elimination.'

Le Temps burns his hand on the barbecue, says a bad word and gives Big Ben the bull's-eye stare.

'How do you spell "sheep", Ben?' He pauses. 'As I thought, you have NO idea. No idea at all. And I think you'll find the correct term is "mutton".'

'He wouldn't know that.' I find my mouth speaking before my brain has caught up. I'm angry with Le Temps for humiliating Big Ben. He can't help being dyslexic.

'Hot potatoes! Hot potatoes!' sings the Triple M teacher like he's selling vegetables in the market and the background noise of the barbecue is his bassline. I turn away from Le Temps to get my jacket potato. I'm starving. But as I leave I can hear Big Ben still guessing.

'Is it hedgehogs?'

∞

We eat the cake indoors because the food has begun to get soggy. Maria dropped her burger on the ground and swore in Portuguese so she got away with it like she always does. We have to take our boots off and leave them at the entrance to the Common Room. I'm worried someone might steal my boots and throw them down the toilet because that happened at my primary school, but Mrs C Eckler says everyone here is well behaved.

The 2048 cake is set up on a large circular table in the middle of the room. It's fully white-iced and decorated with the cupcakes we made earlier. I want to take a photo on my TwentyTwenty so I can look at it forever but don't want the grown-ups to know

I still have it. I'll have to memorise it in my brain. Millennia gives a speech about the importance of leap birthdays. She says some bissextiles choose to celebrate their in-between birthdays on the 28th of February or the 1st of March and that is OK. But some bissextiles only celebrate the leap birthday once every four years. That makes it more special. I know from the way she says it that Millennia's like me. She only celebrates on the true day.

'Today is special. Here at the Time Squad, we drink a toast to time and we eat this cake to acknowledge our rare Gift. Ladies and gentlemen, boys and girls, please raise your glasses . . . TO TIME.'

'To Time!' we say in unison.

'1 minute, 20.95736793 seconds,' says Big Ben, meaning the length of Millennia's speech.

They play the song 'Celebration', which came out in 1980. In 1980, the Olympics were in Moscow and America boycotted them, so Allan Wells won the 100 metres in 10.25 seconds, the slowest time in modern history. Allan Wells was 28 years old, really old for a sprinter. His wife was his trainer. I watched his race online 100 times.

Some of the teachers start dancing on the rugs. Season begins to cut the 'two' cake and Mr C Eckler helps serve everybody. It's the best cake I ever tasted. I'm going to make one when I get back to 2020 and celebrate with Grandma. I think she would like it. Big Ben eats three pieces but nobody minds. It's a very big cake.

Big Ben asks me to go to a midnight feast but I say no because midnight feasts are forbidden and we're not allowed in the boys' chalet. He shows me all the food he's smuggled from the barbecue. It's mainly steak in white rolls. I think he's still wanting to guess what it is, to get a ride in the Ferrari, so maybe they'll do that at midnight. Even though they'll be breaking the rules, I don't blame them for having their own party. After all, we only celebrate our birthdays once every four years. Four years is a long time to wait before the next celebration. Why not make the 29th of February last as long as possible?

Chapter 11:00

THE RED HAT

Big Ben, Ama and I are in The Beanstalk having breakfast whilst everyone else is still in bed. Season's set up breakfast, apologised and gone to lie down in the Common Room. Ama likes what she calls the Human Touch, home-cooked food served by a real person. At her school, it's all done by robots. You get assigned one but never see it. You text your order in advance and collect it from a hatch in the wall. The food lacks soul. But the worse thing's when your robot's having a bad day.

'Texts me stuff like DON'T EAT FISH AND CHIPMUNKS. FISH ARE FORBIDDEN AND CHIPMUNKS ARE FULL OF FAT. I block it some days. Once it put gravy on my sponge pudding. Probably revenge.'

'So they're like a person?' I think of Mange-Tout slapping meat onto the barbecue.

'Yeh. And no. Hates being ignored. Strange thing is,' she puts her head to one side, 'I'm missing them.'

I'm eating porridge made with water, topped with almond

cream. Ama's eating a vegan pain au chocolat and Big Ben has a full English: rootveg rashers, hash browns, beancakes and baked beans. That's one too many bean things. I won't sit too close to Big Ben today.

Big Ben says they had a great midnight feast. They smuggled so much food they couldn't eat it all so they'll supplement the vegan menu with all that meat. They stayed up till 3 a.m.! In our chalet, we all got to bed just after midnight, except Noon, who came back really late, but she's allowed because she's 4-leap. I stayed up all night reading my Bob Beamon book. I read it under the covers with the light from my TwentyTwenty like I do at home in case Grandma comes into the sitting-room to tell me to 'go to sleep-o'. Once I start reading a good book, I can't stop. Bob Beamon talked about how he was a criminal until he realised he was good at the long jump. Maybe MC^2 should read the book so he can learn to be good at something and not be a criminal any more.

Ama finishes her croissant and looks at me for a long time. Then she looks at Big Ben and says:

'Fiona's looking good this morning. Think the rain cleaned her off.'

Big Ben leaps up and goes to the window. Ama lowers her voice.

'Can we trust him?'

'What?'

'To keep a secret?'

I nod my head. Big Ben's very good with secrets. He never told Grandma I read all the Harry Potter series under the covers with the light from my phone. That said, he's only met Grandma twice. Ama walks over to the window and says something to Big Ben. He comes back to our table. She did well making him stop looking at his new carfriend.

'This is top secret,' she says. 'Promise you'll tell no one!'

We nod.

'I'm here to find my brother,' she says. 'He went missing last leap day when he was 3-leap. I'm sure he came here. To this centre.'

'Did he leap and refuse to come back?' I say.

She gives me a hard stare. 'Millennia made it sound like Leaplings were runaways. But Kwesi wasn't like that.'

'You should tell the police,' I say. 'If someone goes missing, they send sniffer dogs to sniff them out.'

'We did,' she says, 'but obviously we couldn't tell them he was going on a Time Squad trip. Or had The Gift. They searched the local area, then stopped looking after a week.'

'But it's their job to find him.'

'They can't time travel, Elle. Kwesi's super bright but a bit wild. He's nonverbal ASD and gets frustrated when people can't understand his signing. He'd already been in trouble with the police. Graffiti mostly. He talks in paint. Looks like his stuff's coming out of the wall. But they made him whitewash his murals. Think they were glad he was out of their hair.'

If I talked in paint, I'd use different shades of white but I bet Kwesi loves bright colours.

'Did he go to a specialist school to help with communicating?'

'Yeh. Where he swapped the term nonverbal for visual. Says

Visual ASD's a better fit.' She smiles and takes a sip of marigold tea. I tried it earlier and spat it out. Disgusting. Like drinking a flowerbed.

'Does his name begin with the letter L?' I say, and Ama jerks her head as if I slapped her.

'How did you . . .' She shakes her head quickly. 'No. His name's Kwesi. Means born Sunday. But we nicknamed him Leapfrog. He was county champion at triple jump.'

'Did he do the long jump?' I say.

'That too.'

Big Ben and I ask at the same time, 'What was his PB?'

'5 metres 90.'

Big Ben shuffles in his chair. '89.49% for a 3-leap.' he says. Some people don't call him Big Ben. They call him The Human Calculator. But they're wrong. He's not a human calculator, he's a human who's super good at maths.

'Was he training for the Olympics?' I say.

Ama rolls her eyes anticlockwise. 'That's irrelevant. He went on Leap 2100 four years ago and never came back.'

'Leap 2100 doesn't exist,' says Big Ben, without pausing. 'It's not a leap year.'

'What?'

'2000 was leap. The next century leap year's 2400. Century leap years have to divide by 400, not four. The maths has to fit.'

Big Ben's right. 1900 wasn't a leap year either. Or 1800, or 1700. The previous centurial leap year was 1600. Ama wouldn't know because she doesn't study PPF. She probably studies history. Or maybe they don't do history in 2048. Maybe they only study the present. She does something funny with her forehead so it's parallel lines like a school exercise book.

'So he lied?'

'He must have invented an itinerary. That's a lot of work,' I say. But inventing something that isn't true is still a lie.

Ama shakes her head. 'He never brought letters home from school. He rarely went to school. Just remember him texting me that he was going on Leap 2100. Maybe it was code for something.'

'Did you keep the text on your phone?'

She shakes her head. 'I didn't think it was important at the time.'

For a split second I remember deleting SOS L but I try not to think about it.

'As Leap 2100 can't exist, maybe he was pretending to leap. Or wasn't sure which year he was leaping to.'

I'm surprised the words I'm thinking in my head are coming out of my mouth. Ama's staring at me again. She takes a sip of her tea but makes a face like she finally realises she's drinking a flowerbed.

'How did you know his tag was a letter L? For Leapfrog.'

'What's a tag?'

'A graffiti signature. They all have one so people know it's them. Kwesi was proud of his art. How did you know, Elle?'

'I didn't.' This is difficult. I'm trying not to think about deleting SOS L but I can't help it. Maybe it was Kwesi who sent me the SOS message from 2048 and signed it L. Maybe he leapt from his Leap 2044 school trip to 2048.

'How do you know he came HERE?' I say.

'Why did you ask if his name began with the letter L?' She's raised her voice. She looks angry and sad at the same time.

I stare down at my bowl of cold porridge. I don't know what to do. I'm scared that Ama doesn't want to be my friend any more. I want to tell her about SOS L but when I open my mouth, nothing comes out. I stare down at my bowl of cold porridge. Ama is definitely angry now.

'Elle. Look at me. If you know something, tell me. If you don't, it's the same as lying!' Her eyes are wet. Maybe she's going to cry.

I don't want to make Ama cry but I'm scared that Kwesi sent a message to me and he got killed in the future and Ama won't be my friend any more. My head hurts from thinking about it. Too many thoughts. Too much.

I stand up and walk out of the café, along the corridor to the other end of the building. The door to the Common Room is slightly open. I walk in. I don't want to talk to GMT or Noon back in the chalet. Not that Noon says very much at all. Season's stretched out on a sofa, fast asleep. The centre table still has the white cloth from last night, covered in cake crumbs. I lift the cloth and sit down under the table. This = having my own special tent. I wish we were camping and not staying in Hive 1. Hive 1 has too many smells in it, deodorant, hairspray, Noon's Chanel No. 5 perfume. But the boys' chalet probably smells of that hair gel Martin Aston uses, so I'm glad I'm not staying there.

I sit for half an hour until my head stops hurting. I hear the door creak and voices. Le Temps and Millennia. The voices go away. I take out my phone and check in case there are more messages. Nothing. I'm not sure my TwentyTwenty's working in 2048. Season has a coughing fit. Then there's a strange gurgling noise. She's being sick. I'm scared she's going to choke but I can't speak or move. She swears and I'm shocked but I don't say anything. Adults sometimes swear if they hit their hands with a hammer. Then it's permissible. I'm not sure you're allowed to swear because you're vomiting. Maybe Season was poisoned by her own beanburgers!

Then I hear slow footsteps coming into the room and Millennia's voice.

'Mrs S, what in the name of Time are you doing?'

Season mumbles something I can't quite hear but it sounds like she's shuffling around on the sofa.

'Oh my word!' says Millennia. 'We need to get this place cleaned up. We don't want one of the Leapers to—'

'If you really cared about the Leaplings, you'd close the centre.'

'I beg your pardon?'

'You didn't inform Intercalary International. Or the local schools. It looks like a cover-up. Do you really think they'd have put pupils at risk? How many more need to go missing? You let Le Temps talk you into . . .' Season can't find the right word.

'Enough! Leapers who break rules put THEMSELVES at risk. The schools are at liberty to leave if they cannot trust their pupils. This is neither the time nor the place for such a discussion. See me in my office at 10:30!'

And I hear Millennia's footsteps leaving the room.

I'm scared to breathe in case Season hears me and thinks I hid here on purpose. I no longer feel scared and sad. My mouth is a capital O with shock. Season didn't want us to come here. Season wanted to keep us safe. Season is good. But Millennia and Le Temps, they wanted us to face danger. Millennia and Le Temps are BAD. It must have something to do with SOS L. It must.

∞

Mrs C Eckler finds me at 9 a.m. Season has gone back to the kitchen. I hear other voices in the room: Ama, Big Ben, GMT. The Mind Full workshop must have started and I'm supposed to be in their group.

'Elle,' she says. 'It's Mrs Eckler. Are you there?'

I don't answer. I hope by not answering she'll know to leave me alone. But she doesn't give up. I can tell by her voice she's much closer than before when she speaks again. Her words come out faster than usual and a bit out of breath, like she's been running.

'It's OK to stay here till you feel better. But I need to see you to know you're safe. That's my job on this trip. I must do my job.'

She's right. I like people who do their job properly. Not like the police, who wouldn't look for Kwesi for more than a week.

'Elle, if you want me to lift the tablecloth to check on you, knock once on the table. If YOU want to lift the cloth, knock twice.'

I pause before knocking twice. I shuffle forwards on my bottom as I'm sitting cross-legged and lift the cloth. She lowers her head, then gets onto her knees to check. When she sees I'm OK, she smiles. Maybe Ama told her about Kwesi and she was worried I'd gone missing too.

'Elle, Ama wants to talk to you. Is that OK?' she says. 'Knock once for yes, and twice for no.'

I knock twice. I don't want to talk to Ama because she shouted at me and doesn't want to be my friend.

'Elle, will you let Ben talk to you?'

I knock once. I don't lift the cloth, though. He can talk to me through the cloth. It's like a veil. It makes me feel safe and I don't have to look at people's faces to see whether their eyes are rolling clockwise or anticlockwise if I say something rude.

'Am I your boyfriend?' he says.

'No,' I say.

When I'm tongue-tied, talking to Big Ben is like talking to Grandma. Sometimes when I'm tongue-tied I only talk to them. If it's Armageddon like after I got SOS L, I don't talk to anyone. There's a gap before he speaks again. Even though I can't see him, I imagine him screwing up his face to think of the next sentence. He'd rather talk totally in numbers.

'Do you want my hat?' he says.

'OK.'

Big Ben gives me objects when I'm sad. Lots of people find that weird but I like it because if the object's soft, I can stroke it. Enjoy its texture. The crumpled red hat appears under the folds of the cloth. It still has mud and twigs on it. At least it doesn't smell too bad. Just of the earth and Big Ben's hair. I hold it in my hand. It's dry, bristly with the caked-on mud, but some areas are still soft. I stroke the soft bits. It's like an animal that ran away for a week and came back, skinny and covered in mud but bits of it still soft and warm. I don't know where that thought came from. I stroke the hat. It's comforting. I turn it inside out. The inside is red fleece and there's a white label with black writing on it. 100% bamboo, waterless wash 20°C, SAVE THE PLANET.

But over the top of the print there are handwritten words. It reminds me of when I want to say two sentences at the same time and it's so overwhelming I end up saying nothing. On top of SAVE THE PLANET, three words written in faded black biro.

Kwesi Atta Asante.

The missing boy.

Chapter 12:00
THE UNDERSTORY

'You can pick these.'

Season's giving us a tour of the grounds. It's the tour that should have taken place yesterday but it was raining and we made birthday cake instead. All 12 of us are here, plus Mr C Eckler, as Mrs C Eckler meditates on a Sunday. I feel guilty hearing that, because I promised Grandma I would pray on Sunday, as our church doesn't exist in 2048, but I haven't done it yet. I'll do it after this tour, back in the chalet, not aloud like Grandma but quietly in my head. It shouldn't take more than half an hour.

There's light rain but it's mild and you can smell the grass. I love the smell. The tour was supposed to be done by Le Temps but he's busy dealing with An Emergency. Maybe one of the cows has run loose and is pooing all over the paths! We're walking so slowly we're almost going backwards. I'm glad Big Ben and I ran yesterday. It was much more fun. Season's teaching us about foraging – free food you can pick in the wild. And the understory – the part of the forest under the shade where things grow in the damp, like mushrooms. She's telling us which ones we can pick and which ones will kill us.

'Have you killed anyone by mistake?' says Jake.

Season laughs. 'Not that I know of. Some of them make you nauseous but most of them won't kill you.' She holds out her bag and we throw in some pink mushrooms with black stems that Season calls Velvet Shanks. They look poisonous but they're not.

'Do any of them make you throw up?' I say.

'The bolete might but they're too bitter to . . .' She frowns at me as if she only just realised what I said. I find my mouth speaking before my brain tells me to stop.

'Is that why you threw up this morning?'

She shakes her head like I'm talking nonsense. 'That wasn't mushrooms, that was too much rich food. I'm usually careful but once every four years . . .' She shrugs her shoulders.

We're walking the same route Big Ben and I took yesterday until we get to the steep path on the left. There's a cordon across it, yellow-and-black-striped, like crime tape. Jake starts to fiddle with it and Season goes still as a statue.

'We can't go that way. It's too dangerous.'

'Did someone get killed?'

'No. Something to do with the path. Le Temps is dealing with it.'

As we continue down the path, I drop back with Big Ben, Ama and GMT. We told GMT about Kwesi after lunch as she's in our group and older than us so she might know something. She went very quiet.

'Weird vibes happen. But Leap 2100?' she shook her head. 'Thought '68 was far out. Some years are clean outta synch.'

'What's that in English?' Ama finds GMT difficult to understand. I only understand one word out of three but I love her speaking like song lyrics. Better than talking in tongues in our church.

'Leap years that ain't leap, dudes disappear. Like a Black Hole.'

'Black Hole, black magic. Why is everything spooky always BLACK? You think Kwesi's in another universe?' Ama gave her the bull's-eye stare.

'No idea. Just, 2100's spooked. In space–time. You leap, end up some year else. Your luggage lost en route, your Chrono gets a glitch, texts flip to the wrong time.'

That might explain why I got the text. Maybe it wasn't a Predictive but a text that went to the wrong time and place. But I didn't say anything. The hat brought my voice back but I hadn't found the right time to tell them about SOS L.

'Did you ever meet my brother?' Ama said.

'Meet him? I KNOW him. Free spirit. Speaks with his hands. But I never heard him talk about Leap 2100. I'll ask MC. He's omniscient.'

'What?'

'Knows everything, everyone, everyplace. If he don't know, I'll eat my hat.'

I hope her hat isn't covered in mud and twigs!

∞

Now, the four of us stop at the junction.

'That's the path we took yesterday. Where we found the hat.'

Ama looks like she's patting an invisible dog with her hand. 'Keep your voice down, Elle. Chat later, yeh.'

It's hard to know when to speak and when not to speak. When to be loud and when to be quiet. It's not 2048 that's outta synch. It's me. I wonder whether I'll ever learn how to say the right things at the right time. Getting it wrong makes me so angry. When Big Ben gets so angry that he has a meltdown, he throws chairs. I've never thrown a chair, though I feel like doing it ten times a day.

Maybe when I think I'm sad or scared, really I'm angry. I should have gone to the Mind Full workshop this morning. It was run by the E-College-E teacher with purple hair who teaches philosophy. They learnt how to empty your mind, how to breathe when you feel angry. You have to count and hold on to each second, day, month, year. I need to learn how to do that.

But sometimes I'm happy.

Big Ben's been holding my hand for the last half-hour, like I'm a little child and would get lost if he didn't. Or maybe he feels lost, like a child. He wasn't like that yesterday; he was happy to run. I smile at him. 'That was nice but I don't want to hold hands any more.' He nods, and walks on ahead with Ama. I look up at the trees and feel the drazzle on my face. Is this really happening, 2048, or has it not happened yet? Is 2020 really the present or do we just think it is?

We've stopped to look at a different type of mushroom that could kill you. They have very long stalks and purple heads speckled with white dots. They're more like flowers than mushrooms. GMT comes over to me.

'You all right, kid?'

'I'm ok.'

'Really?' she says.

'Maybe,' I say.

'What's bugging you?' She sees me frown and carries on. 'You don't have to TELL me. You could text.'

Text? Maybe she knows. I shake my head. I'm not going to text GMT about SOS L. But I like her. The sound of her voice is a warm shower. I think of something to say that relates to time. She's an expert on time.

'If we're in 2048 now, what happens when it really IS 2048?'

GMT sits on a tree stump. 'Ever heard of multiple futures?' I shake my head and she continues. 'The future's a story we're constantly rewriting. Every second someone in 2020 does something, it changes the future. Every nanosecond.' I think of Big Ben when she says that word. 'There's an infinite number of futures.'

I don't like the idea of all those futures. Too much to get my head round and the thought that ANYTHING could happen. Maybe that's why they keep changing the timetable here, why they can't predict the weather. Maybe someone will do something the next second in 2020 and there'll be an earthwave or a heatquake here. Or maybe we won't exist at all. I don't want to think about it. But GMT does.

'Think about it. Everything you do now affects the ever after.'

'But NOW is the 1st of March 2048, 3 p.m. How can that affect things if it hasn't happened yet?'

'We're bissextiles. For us, time's not linear, it's all over the joint. We can change things any place, any time. It's a Gift from God.'

I'm not sure Grandma would agree. She tells me to keep quiet about my birthday, pretend I was born on the 1st of March. But I think she's secretly proud of my Gift. She knows I can use it to do something good. Maybe the good thing is telling the group about SOS L. If Kwesi sent it, we could help him. He may be hiding here in the grounds and will send the text in two days' time. Or maybe he already sent it in another version of the future and I received it and it won't happen again. Either way, I have to tell the others. Not here. Not now. But soon.

I'm thinking this whilst GMT's talking. Telling me how she got too obsessed with the two watches, spent her whole time checking the time rather than seizing the day. *Carpe diem.* Where have I heard that before? Right now, it's the 1st of March 2048, 3:01 p.m. I'm alive. Breathing fresh air, smelling the grass, the mushrooms, GMT's petunia oil. And she's still talking like a song lyric.

'Tomorrow never happens, man. Don't live for tomorrow, live for now. Whenever now is.'

∞

Big Ben, GMT, Ama and I are in the Common Room before dinner, talking about the hat. Big Ben and I are on the sofa, Ama's crouched in a chocolate-brown beanbag and GMT's lying on a rug. Ama thinks Kwesi dropped it deliberately. As a clue.

'He didn't have time to graffiti his tag, so he left that instead.'

'Not logical,' says Big Ben. 'He didn't know we'd see it.'

'Big Ben's right. It doesn't make sense.' My tummy feels like I have a clenched fist in it. I've been thinking all day about SOS L, ever since I saw the writing in the hat. 'Maybe he sent a message to someone.'

Ama gives me the bull's-eye. She has a way of staring, that girl, like a teacher about to exclude you.

'Elle. Sorry I shouted this morning,' she says.

Oops. A nice one. I've almost forgiven her but I like that she said sorry. She wiggles about in the beanbag till she's sitting more upright. Maybe she wants to be my friend again.

'Do you know something? Speak, Elle. I won't be cross. Promise!'

Speak? I want to speak but the words are buzzing round my head like bees. If I tell her about SOS L, she might get cross again. Or people could trace my illegal solo leap via my phone after I got the text and I might get arrested and never get back to 2020, and Grandma won't have anyone to prepare her pepper soup. But if I don't tell her, someone could die and it would be all my fault. The buzzing stops but the words are still moving. I know once they stop moving I'll have to say what I see in my head. The words stop moving.

'I got an SOS.'

Someone takes a deep breath. I don't know who. But the room's gone quiet, like everyone else did the same thing. If they don't breathe out, they'll die. I know they're all staring at me. I know it, even though I'm looking at the floor.

'On your phone?' says Ama.

'Yes.'

'What did it say? Is it still on your phone?'

'SOS L,' I say to the floor. 'I deleted it.'

'You did WHAT?!' Ama starts pacing. I'm sad I told her now. She's going to start shouting at me. GMT walks over to the settee and sits down beside me.

'Chill out,' she says, looking up at the ceiling. 'We don't need to see it. Elle doesn't lie.'

'No. She's just good at concealing the truth,' Ama says quietly.

I shuffle away from GMT on the sofa. The smell of petunia oil is too strong. Big Ben holds out his hand for me to take but I shake my head. Ama takes a deep breath, like she's about to push out of the blocks for the 100 metres.

'Can you remember the phone number?' Her voice is odd, like she's reading the sentence out loud and she just learnt to read, each word an effort. At least she's not shouting.

'No. It wasn't on my list. It was someone I didn't know. I thought they might be a criminal.'

Ama puts her head in her hands. Big Ben says, to the floor: 'When did you get it?'

'The 27th of February 2020. In double geography. Pete LMS

snatched my phone from my hand and read out SOS L to the whole class. I thought he sent it.' I start to cry.

'Sent by a criminal AND someone in your class. Which one? Can't be both.'

Ama's walking round the room now, going round and round in circles. I wish she'd sit down, she's making me dizzy.

'Impossible is nothing,' says GMT. That's on a poster of Muhammed Ali, a boxer-poet, on the wall of our athletics club. 'Coulda been both.'

'Then there would have been two texts, not one,' says Big Ben.

'I meant the person in your class coulda been a criminal,' says GMT.

'Pete LMS? He's too young. But he IS a bully,' I say.

'MC^2 was a criminal at 12,' says Big Ben, and GMT rolls her eyes clockwise 360°. I think she's in love with MC^2.

'MC's no more a criminal than my cat.'

I imagine a burglar dressed as a cat with a long black tail, leaping through time, stealing watches. A cat burglar.

Ama's still walking round the room. Her eyes are shiny with damp and her cheeks are wet.

'Kwesi's missing and you're talking bullies and crims. Wake up, Leaps!'

But we're not asleep. I wish I WAS asleep, the cover pulled over my head, the world disappeared.

The room's gone quiet again. You can hear the weather trying to get in through the windows. Ama stops pacing, then starts again. Big Ben looks out the window.

'What date was it sent?'

'Sent Tue 3 Mar 2048. 23:00.' I'm replaying the image of the text in my head.

'Two days' time,' says Big Ben. 'It hasn't happened yet.'

'Yes, it HAS. I got the text last Thursday.'

'Sent from the future,' says Big Ben. 'So it's not fixed. It's a Predictive. Only the text is fixed.'

It's GMT's turn to get up and walk round the room. Except she doesn't walk in a circle, she walks up and down. At some stage, she and Ama will crash into each other. She talks as she walks.

'We got time. We got the power to change it. I'll tell MC. You just gotta be prepped, Elle. You'll be cool.'

'Two days,' says Big Ben. 'And six hours.'

'To save my brother,' says Ama.

She's convinced Kwesi sent the text. I'm not so sure but I don't say anything. Now's the wrong time to speak. But just now was definitely the RIGHT time to speak. SOS L was a storm in my head and now I've let it out, like releasing the tightest cornrow into the biggest, yellowest, sunniest afro ever. I received a Predictive and Predictives don't lie. SOS L is going to happen and it's going to happen on my TwentyTwenty. I don't know how but I do know when.

I'm ready.

Like on the starting line for the 100 metres. You kneel on the track and settle into your blocks. You rise when they say 'set', but you have to wait for the gun. Sometimes they make you pause for ever but jump the gun and you're out. I could leap two days ahead, I feel so ready. But no. I must wait. You have to wait for the nanosecond the gun goes off and the trick is, when you hear the gun, to run like a bullet. Like it's life and death.

∞ Chapter 13:00 ∞

RITE OF PASSAGE

I know what's going to happen tonight. Storytelling. I LOVE the pattern of stories: you start with a problem and you have to solve it before the end. Bob Beamon's story started with him being born and his mother dying and no one wanting to claim him in the hospital. He had a hard life because he was black and poor and couldn't read. But 8 metres 90 changed his life. It didn't happen straight away. It took time. He said if you don't succeed the first time, you have to try again and again, until you get it correct.

The most important thing about a story is WHEN it happens. When Bob Beamon did his jump, it had to be that exact moment otherwise he could have done a foul or gone from 0 to 10 and been disqualified from the Olympics for swearing, or jumped 8 metres 50. Instead he jumped ahead in time because no one jumped that far for 23 years. That's why Bob Beamon's an honorary Leapling.

Tonight, we're doing storytelling by the campfire with the criminal MC^2 who speaks in rhyme. I don't know why he's called it Twice Upon a Time instead of Once Upon a Time. He does like speaking in riddles.

∞

There's a minor Oops. The session's being run by MC^2 AND Le Temps. Le Temps says he has to be here in case one of us Leapers decides to take off into the future on a whim and besides, it's his job to look after the fire. He mumbles something about Health and Safety and rolls his eyes clockwise 360°. I don't think he likes Health and Safety very much. He prefers Death and Danger.

He takes us to a clearing in the woods. Mrs C Eckler comes too. I'm surprised to see her here because I thought she'd still be doing her meditating, which is taking a deep breath like you're going to run the 100 metres and humming ommmmmmmmmmmmmmmmm. We haven't been to this part of the woods before. When we get there, Noon says one word:

'Beautiful.'

All the trees have been planted in a circle and carved into chairs so we can sit down as an audience. The trees have lots of rings on the bark. That means they're old. You can tell the age of a tree by the number of rings. I look at the tree opposite more closely. It can't be. A symbol. Unmistakeable. ∞. The infinity sign. The sign of MC^2's tattoo. And it isn't just one tree that has it. It's three!

We sit in a circle like we're going to leap but we don't hold hands. The fire is in the middle and it's not raining. This is fun. I like the smell of the smoke and the spitting noise the fire makes when you put logs on it. Not that we're allowed to put anything on the fire. Le Temps does that.

At 7 p.m. exactly, MC^2 appears at the edge of the circle. He's wearing the same outfit he wore to our school, the top and jeans with writing on.

'Greetings to The Round,' he says.

He leads a voice warm-up. We have to say our names, then everyone claps the rhythm of the name. When I say Elle Bíbi-Imbelé Ifíè, some people get it wrong.

Then he says he's going to drop a rhyme about storytelling. When he was in school, everyone said he had no imagination. But he thinks he's got the best imagination of all.

'Cos I had the A the D the H and the D, peeps made fun of me. Had to magic a better world. Had to write my own story.'

Big Ben puts up his hand.

'What if you can't write but you liked writing numbers?'

'It don't matter,' says MC^2, 'whether it's words, numbers, pictures, symbols. $x+y=z$. Beginning, middle, end. Whether it's writ or spit, it's still lit. Literature hatched on the lip. Story's about sequence. Chronology. Repetition.'

I put up my hand. 'Is that why you called it Twice Upon a Time?'

'Yeah. The best stories got echoes, chimes, doubles. Leaps an' Annuals like that spit.'

We all look at Mrs C Eckler, wondering how she's going to

react. But she's just staring at MC^2 like she's hypnotised. It's OK for MC^2 to swear because he's a tutor but we're not allowed, even though it's outside school. Le Temps is nodding his head like he likes the swearing. MC^2 disappears, appears on the spot.

'Rite o' Passage,' he says, 'is how the best tales hang. Most of you just gone 2-leaps to 3-leaps. Some just done your first fast-forward in the deep blue. When you do something big you ain't done before, that's Rite o' Passage.'

Big Ben puts up his hand again.

'What if you can't write?'

He thinks MC^2 said Write a Passage, like in school where Big Ben has an assistant to write the words down. But a Rite of Passage is like in Kenya when boys have to wrestle a lion to the ground to prove they're a man and not a boy any more. I don't know what the girls have to do but I'm glad I'm not a boy in Kenya. The lion would win.

'Nothin' to do with writing, Ben. I'm talking R I T E. Something you do to show you've learnt something hard, risen to the challenge, grown up.' He seems to double in size. 'Gimme a fairytale an' I'll drop a freestyle.'

We all go quiet till we all speak at once: *Babes in the Wood, Little Red Riding Hood, Beauty and the Beast, Hansel and Gretel*. I picture them written one on top of the other. It looks a mess.

'OK, gimme a split,' he says, closing his eyes tight like clenched fists. 'Listen up, peeps! Twice 'pon a time, the megamix.'

'Leap in The Round an' you'll never be seasick,
don't lose your hood or your hat for the scenic,
paint the trees red an' you'll end up anaemic;

stay on the path, face the wolf and defeat it,
sunny day night, don't drop bread, birds will eat it,
witch wants you fat, it's a fact, don't delete it;

house made of toffee and pear drops and d-mix,
mouth of the oven flared up like a phoenix,
the fee-fi-foe . . .'

'Bravo!' says Le Temps, clapping with his huge hands. 'Pure genius! Give him a round of applause; he deserves it.'

We do as we're told. But I don't like MC^2's poem because it mixed up lots of fairy tales. Maybe megamix means you mix up lots of stories, pile them up one on top of the other till they look a mess. And there was no end! He didn't tell us about Jack and the Beanstalk. And we never found out what happened to Hansel and Gretel. In the original version, the witch fattens up Hansel to roast him but Hansel pretends he's still thin, so when the witch opens the oven to roast GRETEL, Gretel puts the witch in the oven instead. I don't think Ama liked the poem much either. When everyone else is clapping, she has her hands stuck together like she's praying.

Le Temps helps us roast marshmallows by the fire. It doesn't take very long and some of them go gooey. There are pink ones and white ones. Mrs C Eckler offers me the white ones, which are burnt on the outside and runny in the middle but they taste good. I have six! Then Mrs C Eckler brings us mugs of hot milk.

After that, MC^2 asks us to take an object out of our bags. I take out my white afro comb. Lots of people take out their Chronophones but MC^2 says they should all be different objects to make the story work. I thought Big Ben would take out his new stopwatch but he takes out a white bread roll with meat in from the night before. He looks like he's going to eat it and I tell him not to. It might make him sick or die.

The game is to tell a group story. We each have to say a sentence in the story, including the object we took out of our bag. MC^2 has a pen and he begins:

'Once upon a time, a boy wrote a message on a tree.'

Lots of pupils find it difficult and say sentences that don't make sense to the story. They all manage to include their objects, though. I'm pleased with my sentence, which is:

'His afro comb was white as a tomb.'

I'm proud because comb and tomb is an eye rhyme and MC^2 high-fives me.

'Maestro, Elle!'

Once the game's finished, Le Temps takes Big Ben's roll and throws it on the fire for Health and Safety reasons.

'Hope you haven't got any more of those in your schoolbag,' he says. 'We don't want you getting ill.'

Big Ben doesn't answer, which either means he doesn't want to talk to Le Temps because he doesn't like him or he DOES have more in his bag but isn't going to lie. Or both.

∞

Back in our chalet, Ama's pacing the bedroom. GMT's already in bed. Noon's still out – I think she prefers being outside to in. She's fallen in love with The Round. Maybe she likes the trees with the infinity symbols on them. Ama's forehead is so scrunched up she looks like somebody else. I don't like her looking like an old person when she's 14. I want to look away but I keep glancing at her sideways.

'He knows something.'

'Who?' I say.

'MC^2. Don't lose your hat, paint the trees red. He's giving us a message.'

'He saw Big Ben wearing the red hat last night,' I said. 'He was freestyling. When you're freestyling you say the first thing that comes into your head.'

'No, Elle. He said sunny day night. He meant Sunday, code for Kwesi. He must have known Kwesi. He—'

'He didn't finish his poem.'

They both look at me and I look away.

'Le Temps started clapping but he hadn't finished. It was a bad poem. It was all mixed up with no proper ending.'

Ama stops in the middle of the room. Her eyes go the biggest I've ever seen eyes.

'Yes! Le Temps stopped him. Thought it was odd. The way he clapped like crazy when the poem was . . . you know.'

GMT sits up in bed. Her hair's frizzy and wild, like she hasn't combed it for days. She claws her fingers and combs it back from her face.

'We may be reading too much into this, guys, but,' she says,

'I've known MC for light years. Brother speaks rhyme or code or rhymecode.'

'He's not brother to you,' says Ama.

'Near as,' says GMT. She begins to climb down the ladder. 'Something's happening here. MC's giving you clues, Elle. Has a sixth sense when he's 'stylin'. It must link with the Predictive. How did the tale end?'

'Gretel throws the witch into the oven,' I say.

'I mean MC's mix. Something about a phoenix?'

'No. It was fee-fi-fo but he never got to fum. Le Temps started clapping. That's *Jack and the Beanstalk* not *Hansel and Gretel.*'

GMT starts pacing the room. Ama's pacing the room. It's not a very big room. I look away. I don't want to witness a crash. GMT stops pacing and Ama walks straight into her. Ama swears but she doesn't sit down. She just keeps on walking. GMT pulls her hair back hard till she looks like a boy again.

'Guys,' she says, 'MC's on to something. The tales, don't you see? They're all about—'

'MC this, MC that! You're obsessed.' Ama rolls her eyes anticlockwise. 'Maybe Season's in on it. She runs The Beanstalk. Maybe SHE'S the wicked witch. Maybe it's me. Maybe it's Elle. Maybe it's YOU! How will this help find Kwesi?' She runs out of the chalet.

But I'm not listening to them shouting any more. I'm thinking about MC^2's rap with too much remixing and no end. Why did Le Temps stop him? Does Le Temps hate fairy tales because he's a witchcraft himself? Maybe this has something to do with the Predictive. MC^2 called me maestro, which means I'm good at storytelling. He wasn't able to finish his story but I could. I wouldn't speak in riddles and rhymes. It wouldn't be fairy tales, it would be real. I have to find out what SOS L means. It's up to me to finish the story. MY story.

Chapter 14:00

THE LAW OF THE JUNGLE

Noon returned to our chalet in the middle of the night and this morning says she has a stomach cramp. She certainly SOUNDS different, not that she talks very much. Mrs C Eckler comes in to make sure she's OK then leaves. I guess since Noon's 4-leap she must be treated like a grown-up. She didn't come here with a school. But she's not telling the whole truth. Her not feeling well has something to do with the time she returned to the chalet. 4 a.m.! Then she spent a whole hour tapping into her phone. Obsessed with texting, that girl. At least she's not wearing that horrible Chanel No. 5!

I'm scared this morning because we have a workshop with Le Temps who might be a witchcraft. But I'm not going to be like Noon and pretend I'm ill. I have to attend because Big Ben will be there and he hates Le Temps. I don't want him to get angry and have a meltdown. If he throws a chair, he might get excluded from Leap 2048. So I won't tell Big Ben that Le Temps is a witchcraft. That can wait till later.

The workshop's taking place in The Round, same as last night. When I tell Noon she'll be sad she missed it. She loves The Round. Thankfully, the seats carved out of cut-down trees are rooted to the ground, so Big Ben won't be able to wrench one out and throw it. We sit in a circle like before. Big Ben's on my left, Ama's on my right. She squeezes my hand hard when we sit down. I don't mind, as I know she's sad about Kwesi. Le Temps clears his throat like people do before they make an important announcement and want you to listen extra carefully.

'Good morning, fellow survivors. Welcome to Law of the Jungle. Please take out your phones.'

We all fumble in our bags. I take out my Chronophone but keep the TwentyTwenty in my bag. I don't want Le Temps to offer to look after it for me. He looks around the circle.

'Turn them off,' he says in his buttery voice. He looks around the circle again and smiles. It's a strange smile, not sure whether it's happy or angry. 'How does it feel with your phone switched off? Anyone?'

You can always count on Jake to say something.

'We can't communicate.'

'Good. Anyone else?'

'We don't know what time it is. Or where we are.' That was Martin Aston aka Aston Martin.

'Exactly. Without your phones, you're lost. Literally. Metaphorically. You don't know what time it is or where you are. You feel cut off from reality. You don't know who you are any more. Without your phone, you cease to exist.'

He looks straight at me and I feel scared. Maybe he knows I kept my phone in my bag.

'This morning, I'm going to teach you survival skills.

'Do you know what time of day it is by looking at the shadows? What time of night by looking at the stars? In the summer? In the autumn. Winter. Spring?

'Do you know the difference between the sun and the moon? What they do? That's why I'm called Le Temps. I understand the weather and time. You all know what climate change is?' We nod. 'I've noted changes over the years. How Mother Nature works. It's all in here and in here.' He thumps his bald head, his large chest. 'Not in here.' He pulls out his Chronophone.

'When I was your age, I kept my brain in my phone. I didn't even know my own number. Turn off my phone, I was a ruddy mess.'

To teach at Leap 2048 you have to pass a swearing test.

Though Le Temps is a witchcraft, I like the first half of the workshop because he makes us look at the sky and the clouds and the trees. It's better than being indoors. One of the exercises, he makes us run in different directions for five minutes and we have to take mental note of landmarks like unusual trees, mushroom clusters, so we can find our way back. It's a bit like Hansel and Gretel leaving a bread trail so they can find their way home, except we don't leave lumps of bread.

We go in pairs and I go with Big Ben. There's no longer a cordon across the steps up to the cow field. Without saying anything to each other, we run up the steps and back to the place we found Kwesi's red hat. A minute later, Ama comes up behind us.

'You're supposed to be with GMT,' I say. 'You'll get into trouble.'

She shrugs her shoulders. 'I needed space. Is this the spot?'

We nod.

There's nothing on the ground. Apart from that, it hasn't changed from last time we were there. No footprints. No clues. Time to go back to the group.

We're back in The Round having the snacks Season gave us this morning, delicious home-made white chocolate chip cookies that melt in the mouth. Le Temps takes out what looks like dried tree bark and starts eating it. I can see it's difficult to chew. Maybe that's where he gets his powers from. It's when I look behind him that I see the tree. ANOTHER tree with the ∞ infinity sign. And another. I look back at Le Temps. He looks like his whole brain has gone into eating the tree bark. He doesn't know about the infinity symbols. Or maybe he does and that's why he's sitting under one of them. I look at the signs again and frown. I can remember exactly where I was sitting last night and how the trees looked. There were DEFINITELY only three symbols last night. Now there are five!

∞

The second half of the workshop, Le Temps kills a rabbit with a gun.

He doesn't warn us, just pulls out his gun and BANG! I'm

not happy he killed the rabbit. He explains that killing wildlife is not the same as cooping up animals in factories, fattening them up just to kill them. It's OK if it's organic. I can't look at the dead rabbit unless I look the other way and squint my eyes. The blood doesn't look red, it looks black. I don't want to look and I do want to look. GMT shouts at Le Temps.

'Murderer! You're teaching kids it's cool to—'

'Bad things happen,' he says. 'I don't shield children from bad things. I prepare them. Law of the Jungle.'

GMT walks out. I'm worried she's going to get excluded, as she didn't ask for time-out. Maybe you don't have to ask for time-out in the future. I'm sad and angry at the same time about the rabbit. When I speak, my voice sounds croaky but I still manage to speak.

'It's not a jungle, it's a country park.'

'WAS,' he says. 'This is my land now.'

'The rabbit didn't deserve to die. It wasn't attacking you.'

'Hare, actually. Totally different species. Welcome to my Garden of Eden.'

He sticks out his tongue and quickly puts it back into his mouth. It's not a very good impersonation of a snake. He did the same thing on the introductory film, only faster. It was so fast you almost couldn't see it. I play the film back in my head. The camera zooms in on the grass and the trees and shows a bald man chopping wood. Then the letters like flies make me dizzy again until they become the caption, 'LE TEMPS, Eco-landscaper', and then Le Temps is a talking head. He says, 'I plan the land.' And something's not quite right, something's out of synch, but

I don't know what it is. It reminds me of something. I have that feeling again. I play the film over and over till my head aches.

Le Temps skins the hare, cooks it on a campfire and offers it around. What Le Temps did was bad but the hare smells nice. Most of the children don't eat it but Big Ben does. So do Jake and Martin Aston. Typical. If Big Ben knew Le Temps was a witchcraft I don't think he'd eat it, but I can't tell him anything at the moment about Le Temps or the infinity signs or the film. There's too much going on in my head.

∞

I don't eat much lunch, although Season's made yam fritters. Her mouth goes into a minus sign. But everyone's being different today. GMT's still angry Le Temps killed the rabbit that was a hare so she's not speaking to anyone. Ama's not speaking to GMT because GMT called MC^2 'brother'. Noon is pretending to have a stomach ache and I'm cross with Big Ben for eating the hare so I'm not speaking to him. I don't want to sit in The Beanstalk any more.

There's half an hour before the afternoon workshop begins with MC^2. I go back to Hive 1 to dry my hair. It was a bit damp outside and my hair never dries on its own. Afro hair's like that. After drying it, I go upstairs for my comb. Noon's sitting up in front of the mirror. I look at her reflection, not at her. She looks ever so slightly different. Everyone looks different in the mirror. No one's totally symmetrical. She turns round to face me and I stare. I know what's changed. Her face looks thinner, you can see her cheekbones. She wouldn't have got thinner overnight.

'You must be Elle,' she says, and I think, of course I'm Elle. You know that. We've been sharing a chalet for two days. Then comes the Oops. It's not a totally bad Oops but it's not a good Oops either. Something's topsy-turvy. She stands up and I notice she's wearing the beige-cream two-tone shoes with a strap across the middle and heels shaped like an hourglass. But she's shrunk by two inches. She's shorter than me in her shoes.

'I'm not Noon. I'm Eve,' she says, 'Noon's twin sister. I've come to find her.'

∞ Chapter 15:00 ∞

EVE

'Wow,' I say. 'Noon and Eve.'

'Yes, Mama went for the bissex names. Noon came first, so she got to be "midday". I arrived so late, Mama thought I'd be an Annual. Imagine. Twins born on different days.'

She sits down on the edge of the bed. It's my bed but I don't mind because I love her name.

'How fast can you run the 100 metres?'

'Run?' she says. 'I can barely walk after the leap. First time I've done an interdecade. Sick as a dog.'

'Was it you in bed this morning? Where's Noon?' I say.

'Yes. Sorry for the French farce. Had to stand in, in case they raised the alarm. Another missing leap. I guess she's with Kwesi. We have an agreement, Noon and I: if she stops texting . . .'

'Why did you say ANOTHER? Do you know about Kwesi?'

'Yes! He told us about leaps going missing. 2100 was a Black Hole.'

That's what GMT said. So there IS something weird about 2100. It must link to SOS L.

'His sister's here. She's called Ama. She's here to find Kwesi but we don't know where to look.' I've forgotten about my hair. This is much more exciting. 'When did you meet him?'

'Paris, '24.'

I'm impressed. Not many people can leap across time to another country! I wonder if he went there to watch the Paris Olympics.

'Did you meet Harold Abrahams?' Harold Abrahams was a British runner who won the 100-metre dash in 10.6 seconds. Maybe they called it the 100-metre dash in those days because they thought runners ran so fast they looked like a dash: —. But they didn't run as fast as sprinters do now.

'No, we met Kwesi in a café in Montmartre. He sold us a Chronophone. Love at first sight for Noon.'

'He shouldn't have done that. That's an Anachronism!'

'Darling, the world RUNS on Anachronisms. Would we progress otherwise? Who do you think invented the internet? Leaps with The Gift.'

She called me darling. Maybe she's a bisexual bissextile. She's prettier than Noon, though they're identical. I try to imagine Kwesi selling Chronophones in Paris, 1924. I don't know what he looks like, but I imagine he looks a bit like Ama but with a shorter afro and much longer legs so he can jump 5 metres 90. He must be brilliant at selling if he's nonverbal.

'Did he talk in paint?'

'Paint? Is that some kind of slang? No, my dear, he talked with his hands.'

'Ama said he was nonverbal.'

'Yes. His Chronophone helped things to flow but Noon understood him. She texts him ten times a day. Never stops talking about him. Kwesi this, Kwesi that. Noon's quiet unless she's around Kwesi. She's dying for a rendezvous.'

That's a French word for a secret date. I like the sound of it on her lips and the way she pouts when she says it. She doesn't say it the English way. She says it like she's French.

'All very innocent. Noon's never had a beau before. Chaperone day and night meant we couldn't meet boys. But the Chronophone helped us keep in touch. She only used it for texting.' She sits down at the mirror. 'Texted me last night to say she'd been offered a job. Wanted my opinion.'

'What job?'

'Eco-something. Noon loves Nature.'

I frown. There's only one person who would offer such a job. Le Temps. Maybe Noon accepted the job and leapt to work in another year. If she did, why didn't she text her sister?

Eve smooths down her short, blonde bob and turns her head from side to side.

'D'you think I'll pass? For Noon?'

'You're too short. Why are you shorter?'

'I was ill as a child so we ate different food. Noon's the strong one. No one will notice if I wear these.' She produces some cream, brown and orange striped platforms.

'You can't wear them, they're GMT's,' I say.

‘Darling, she only wears ’68. Noon’s texted me on all of you. These are ’70s fancy dress for Greenwich Mean Time. Anyway, she doesn’t believe in possessions.’

I don’t think GMT would like Eve saying her full name or wearing her shoes. I’m scared about Eve pretending to be Noon because putting on a disguise is a form of lying. But she’s already put the shoes on. They’re a good fit.

‘Now, I must stop talking,’ she says.

‘Why?’ I want her to keep talking forever. I love the way she talks.

‘I have to make people believe I’m Noon. For the afternoon.’ She smiles at the rhyme. ‘All for a good cause. Will you keep my secret?’

I nod. I hope it’s not lying if I don’t say that Noon is really Eve but I love secrets. Secrets are about not talking. I’m good at that.

Chapter 16:00

MIND OVER MATTER

E=MC² is projected on the floor of The Igloo. The floor's transparent so we can see down into the room below. At first, I'm scared I'll fall through the floor but when no one does I step inside. It looks like walking on ice but doesn't feel slippery at all. The letters move when we tread on them.

We haven't had a workshop in here before. The room's a replica igloo. Even the bricks are large like blocks of snow and the chairs are not chairs but white blocks arranged in a circle. Big Ben would find it hard to throw one of these. We all sit down in our tracksuits. I feel bad that in the excitement I forgot to tell Eve to wear a tracksuit, but one or two of the others have forgotten too, so she doesn't stand out so much. The windows are a circle of light high up in the ceiling. I like this room. I've always wanted to build an igloo but there was never enough snow. You'd have to go to Scotland to find lots and I've never been there.

At exactly 2 o'clock, MC² appears in the middle of the circle.

Some of the pupils cheer but I purse my lips. I know he's going to start talking in riddles.

'Here is some chatter,
prattle an' patter,
'nacular natter:
ice will not shatter,
peeps will learn stratta' —
mind over matter.'

He clicks his phone and it starts to snow. I don't think it's real snow, as the room's not cold enough. I LOVE snow. Every snowflake's different, an infinite number of patterns. Eve starts to shiver. In 1924 they hadn't invented virtual snow. MC^2 clicks his phone and it stops snowing. He did it to show off.

'Some of you came holding hands in a Chrono.
Today, gonna teach you how to leap solo.
Before you leap through time, you gotta learn to
leap through space . . .'

He vanishes from the middle of the circle and reappears a split second later outside it.

'. . . or you'll throw up all over the place.'

So that's what I did wrong. I changed the correct order of things.

'Some of you came by jet without fuel.'

he says, walking back into the middle of the circle,

'Gonna teach you how to leap old skool.'

He taps his phone and $E=MC^2$ vanishes from the centre of the floor and an old film is projected on the walls. The title of the clip is *Leap of the Century*. My heart's beating so fast, I'm scared it'll jump out of my chest. This is it! This is what I play over and over in my head every day of my life till it's part of who I am. Bob Beamon doing the long jump at the Olympics in Mexico City on the 18th of October 1968. The run-up, the leap, the kangaroo-hopping afterwards. It's over in seconds. It doesn't show the long wait before they announced the world record, the measuring with the old-fashioned measuring tape because the modern technology only went to 28 feet.

Robert Beamon jumps and makes sports history. The makers of the measuring instrument never foresaw a jump so staggering.

The film, the commentary, it's like I'm there on the runway, in the moment, leaping through space and time. The best feeling ever. MC^2 must love it too. I know Big Ben and Maria will. I can't wait to discuss it with them.

8 metres, 90 centimetres = twenty-nine feet, two and one-half inches flashes up on the wall followed by a quote from Lynn 'the Leap' Davies, who got the long jump gold medal in 1964.

He has broken the Olympic record by a half-century.

MC^2 blinks his body.

'In 1968, Bob Beamon smashed the world record. World got a new word: Beamonesque. In 1969, man set foot on the moon. Peeps weren't Leaps. Not only Leaps leap. ANYONE can leap. Don't have to be a leap year. Leap's a feat no one at the time could believe. Can be physical, physiological, psychological, logical, lexical.

'To make that leap, you gotta have IMAGINATION.

'Anyone can leap with mindset. Leaps know it. Annuals know it. Why'd they change the school system? So peeps can play to their strengths. E-College-E max the eco. Triple Ms got the motto MIND OVER MATTER. Today, you get the strategy, the funda-mentals. Up to you to apply it.'

He divides us into pairs, each Leapling with an Annual. Leaplings have to leap within the room; Annuals have to coach us and give feedback. In the second half of the workshop, we'll go outside on the field so Annuals can long jump and Leaplings give feedback. You must focus on exactly where you want to land, find a blemish like a crack in the floor, a spot of dirt, a fuzzy tile. Channel your mind into it, imagine you're already there. When you've gone into the zone, count down slowly from 10 to 0 in your head. When you reach zero, you leap.

I'm paired with Ama. She isn't a very good coach since she spends the whole time staring at MC^2. She wants to ask him about Kwesi. Across the room there's a blemish under the floor that looks like ice when it splinters and starts to melt. I hope it doesn't act like real ice. The blemish is beautiful, like a waterlily. I stare and stare at it till my mind leaves my body. My brain's tingling. Maybe that's what meditating is supposed to feel like. When I leapt by mistake at school, I never reached the relaxed stage. I try to count down slowly but my mind is racing from the Bob Beamon film. It comes out like German.

10,9,8,7,6,5,4,3,2,1,zero.

∞

'Elle. Elle!'

Someone's calling my name. I don't recognise the voice. It sounds old and wise. 'ELLE,' it says. I'm scared to open my eyes because I don't know where I am. I know I'm not in the chalet but I feel like I've just woken up. Slowly, I open my eyes. They feel gummed up like when I was little and ill and Grandma would give me pepper soup, which made me cough and get well again.

My eyes are wide open. There's a circle of light above me which forms into windows. I'm still in The Igloo. A face comes into view. Millennia. Another: MC^2. Millennia speaks first.

'Elle. You have recovered. You passed out when you leapt.' Then she lowers her voice so only I can hear. 'Up to your old tricks?'

'Everyone nukes sometime,' says MC^2. 'If they got talent. Your boy freaked maestro. Season sorted him out.'

He means Big Ben, who worries when I get upset so he must have panicked when I fainted.

'What time is it?' I say. My voice doesn't sound like my own, as if it's coming from outside my body.

‘3:22,’ he says. ‘You hit the right spot but went an hour ahead. You’ve only been out a few minutes.’

Millennia helps me sit up. I realise I’m on the ground and try not to look down through the clear floor. They say it was best not to move me in case of complications. I’m starting to feel a bit queasy, from the leap, and Millennia’s words. She thinks she met me before. She must be mistaking me for someone else, someone she hates. I wish she’d go away. I’m scared.

Season enters the room and she and Millennia discuss what happened. Their words are echoing so loud I can almost see them bouncing off the walls. Suddenly my mouth goes dry, my body starts to convulse. I’m going to vomit. As I retch, Season puts a bowl in front of me and I realise there aren’t any sweets in it. She guessed I was going to be sick and brought an empty bowl with her. I hope she has some of her sweets to make me better afterwards.

When I’ve finished, Season helps me to wipe myself clean and gives me a glass of water. She nods at Millennia, who’s standing by the door.

‘I hope you recover sufficiently, Elle. I must attend to the centre.’

Millennia hesitates for a second until I look up at her, then leaves the room. I’m glad she’s gone and she must be glad too. I bet she’s fed up with people being sick all over the place. Season offers me a sweet from her pocket. It tastes of juicy oranges and I feel better immediately. I still don’t want to stand up because I’m scared I’ll be sick if I move. Here, cross-legged on the floor, I don’t feel nauseous at all but I still don’t feel able to speak again. MC^2 raises his thumb to Season. But Season's face has gone white. She doesn't look like Season at all.

'Elle. When you went missing. We were worried you'd—'

'Done an interdecade,' MC^2 finishes her sentence. 'You're prime, Elle. Mind over matter, you could've. Glad you didn't. Season, rest up. It's sorted. Elle needs space.'

They thought I might have leapt to another decade by mistake. Then I'd be much harder to find and they'd have another missing Leap! Season's slowly starting to look like herself. She rises slowly to go. Before she does, she gives MC^2 a handful of sweets. I'm pleased there's only one person here now. Three was too many. I was scared I was going to die and they were standing round my bed like in the olden days. He sits cross-legged on the floor like me.

'Elle, I know stuff's happening.' I open my eyes in surprise and he shrugs his shoulders. 'OK. Greenwich told me you got a Predictive. Knew you was Special. Like Kwesi. Me and him go back decades. We used ta hang all over the timeline but brother went missing, went silent on me. Something's up and I can't work out why. Noon missing since last night.'

I open my mouth but nothing comes out. He knows about the Predictive and Kwesi AND Noon? Did I say something in my sleep?

'Knew soon as the twin walked in with the high-rise feet. Noon don't move like that. Nothing gets past The Squared.' He sways from side to side like he can't stay in one place for too long. 'We SHOULD report it but they won't do nothing.

Noon's 4-leap. Adult. She ain't gone long enough. But we need to act. Eve knows we know. Double-act could help us.'

He stands up like he's about to start rapping again. I hope he doesn't. My brain couldn't stand it.

'Too many Leaps gone missing here.' He shakes his head. 'Time Squad didn't deliver. Kwesi tried to solve it solo. Now he's AWOL. Greenwich says glitch in the anti-leap. She's sharp but she ain't cracked this one.'

'Kwesi told Ama he was going on Leap 2100.'

MC^2 whistles through his teeth. 'First I heard. Greenwich know?'

I nod and he disappears, appears on the spot. He can't help himself.

'Thought she was trying to tell me somethin' last night. We got interrupted.'

I think of Le Temps interrupting his freestyle, Millennia interrupting Season when she couldn't find the right word.

'Season wanted to keep us safe but Millennia and Le Temps want to put Leaplings in danger.'

I tell him about their conversation when I was under the table. He whistles again, this time much longer.

'Don't say I said nothin' but Millennia's past participle. She switched sides. Time Squad used to catch crims every week. Now we're told, wait. Turn a blind eye to small crime: go for the big boss. Problem is, Elle,' he disappears, appears, 'Millennia's the big boss.'

'Millennia? She's pretending to catch criminals when she's HEAD of the criminals?' I knew she was bad but never guessed she was bad to the power of 3. He nods his head.

'We got proof but not enough. Trust me. Leaps are on the case.'

He forms a fist with his left hand. The infinity tattoo: ∞.

'See this? Earned it the hard way. Kwesi the same. Greenwich got one on her ankle. She don't flaunt it. We work for Infinity. Call ourselves The Infinites.'

He disappears, reappears the other side of the room. I look at him out of the corner of my eye without moving my face. He continues:

'Kwesi wanted a Youth League. Thought Time Squad wasn't doin' enough for the planet. Suspected Millennia. Infinity got wind of it and next I knew, I got TWO jobs. I'd ditch Time Squad, but I'm contracted.'

'Have you got a motto?'

'Yeah, sis. ROOT FOR THE FUTURE. We gotta protect tomorrow. Sow the seeds for the planet's needs. Infinites are top secret. Only report to Infinity.' He checks his watch.

'Time's ticking, Elle. Need to step up. I told Eve keep up the act but skip tonight. Film's optional anyways. And lie low tomorrow. She can tell Ama but say nothing to no one else. Wise Old Owl.' He opens a sweet and pops one into his mouth. 'We gotta find Noon. She's phone-dead. Maybes she heard from Kwesi.'

I frown at him eating the sweet. It's like he reads my mind.

'Won't hurt me,' he says. 'Jus' making sure the sweets are sweet. Season's safe but we can't take no chances.'

It must link to the Predictive. Maybe MC^2 detects a crime that hasn't been committed yet. A crime that will be committed at 11 o'clock tomorrow evening. Or a crime that's already been committed in a different future, the future that happened when I was making my speech in school. He offers me another sweet. This time it's cherries. He pauses for a long time and then he speaks.

'I smell an Anachronism. Elle, some advice. You get a Predictive, you're chosen. You gotta act solo. Dial the 2 and the triple 0 on your Chrono.'

∞

For dinner I have braised tofu stew with dumplings. I'm starving. Season gives me a second helping and an extra potato-bread roll freshly baked. I hope she's not fattening me up to eat me. I'm really looking forward to her B(re)aking Bread workshop tomorrow. Ama's speaking more now. She's even talking to GMT! I think she's feeling happy because she knows MC^2 is looking for Kwesi. She tells me about the second half of the Mind Over Matter workshop. It was held outside. The sun was shining, so it was like the 1968 Olympics in Mexico City. The Annuals had to visualise a leap like Bob Beamon did and practise on the grass or, if they preferred, brainstorm a robot. Bob Beamon visualised his winning leap for months before he did it. The Leaplings had to coach them and offer feedback.

Megan Smith jumped 5 metres 26 centimetres. Big Ben worked out that was an 89.45% age grade, similar to Kwesi's.

Maybe they know each other. Megan goes to Triple M. Lots of the pupils there are good at sports. Some of them are good at dancing or gymnastics as well as athletics. Some of them are brilliant at all three: music, movement and maths. Like Ama. She brainstormed a brilliant robot that could speak Akan. I'd like to go to that school because I like sports and I could still learn PPF secretly online. I'm even better at PPF than I am at running.

Ama's sitting opposite me. She had to stop Eve complaining about the food because everyone would realise she's not Noon. Eve's gone back to the chalet to sulk. Noon forgot to tell her there's no meat. This food must look alien compared to 1924. Ama's eating chocolate sponge and custard. It looks and smells amazing but I'm too scared to eat it. I wish I could be more adventurous like Ama. She's making the kind of noises you make when you love the food. Big Ben's on my right. He hasn't left my side since I came to the canteen. I went back to the chalet to lie down a bit after fainting so they didn't see me all afternoon.

'You should have seen Big Ben. HEARD him. He went crazy. Thought you were dead!' says Ama.

'I only fainted,' I say. I don't really feel like talking. Only eating! I break open the roll. It's still warm and the coconut oil melts into it. I take a bite.

Big Ben still looks pale, as if he was the one who passed out, not me. He's hardly eating anything. Not himself at all.

'I couldn't see you. Then they said I can't come in the room.'

'Tried to kick the door down.' Ama laughs. She thinks it's funny. 'He missed the whole outdoor session. MC^2 carried on as normal. He wasn't quite sure how far you'd leapt into the future but he guessed around an hour. "The show must go on," he said.'

'I like him now,' I say. 'Even though he's a criminal. He's trying to help us.'

Big Ben stands up so quickly I'm scared he's going to throw a chair. He starts grinding his teeth.

'Do you want to do running?' I say.

He gives me the glass-eye, still grinding his teeth. His fists are clenched. But why? MC^2 is helping us. Maybe he doesn't know Noon's missing. That Noon is Eve. I want to get a piece of coconut cake but I don't want to leave Big Ben like this. Season comes over, sits opposite him.

'Ben, do you want to see Fiona?'

There's a long, long pause. It looks like Big Ben's gone into a trance. Then he nods his head and slowly follows Season out of the café. A minute later I see them through the glass. Big Ben's sitting in the driver's seat and Season's in the passenger seat. I'm worried he'll start the car and speed off at 200 miles per hour but he doesn't. He just sits in the driver's seat, pretending to drive.

I fetch myself a piece of coconut cake and eat it. Cake makes me think of the leap celebration and the leap celebration makes me think of Grandma. When I get home, it will be the 29th of February 2020 and I'll be able to celebrate my birthday again with Grandma. I'll make Grandma the vegan birthday cake out of coconut cream, white sugar, white flour and lots of baking powder to make it rise. I think Grandma will like it.

∞ Chapter 17:00 ∞

TO BAKE MY BREAD

Today SOS L is going to happen.

I don't know how but I do know when. 23:00. Tuesday, 3 March 2048. Ama thinks Kwesi sent it first time round but we'll never be able to trace the sender because I deleted it. I still don't know. But it definitely wasn't sent by Pete LMS because Pete LMS is in my school in 2020 and he can't leap to 2048 to send the text.

Big Ben still isn't talking to me. I don't know what's wrong with that boy. Today, my heart's like a balled-up fist in my chest, it's so hard to breathe. There've been so many Oopses, I think they should rename this week Oops 2048.

∞

The first Oops is breakfast. My routine is to run before breakfast, then go back to the chalet to shower. This morning, the sky's still red with the sunrise and so foggy I can hardly see Fiona – and she's bright green! I can't see any sky traffic at all. I peer ahead of me. Big Ben isn't standing by Fiona to meet me. His routine is get up and admire Fiona before we go on our run. Before we start running, he always says, 'I'm going to hack into Fiona in drive mode,' and I say, 'No, you're not.' His uncle taught him to drive not fly. I haven't seen him since dinner.

Fiona's parked where she usually is. There's a smoky smell coming from The Beanstalk. You can't usually smell breakfast cooking so strongly. It's a good thing and a bad thing. A good thing because I like the smell, even though it's strong; it smells of salt and fat, it makes my mouth water, and it's a bad thing because it's the smell of meat. Bacon! Surely Season hasn't become a Carnivore overnight!

I go into breakfast with Ama. GMT refuses to enter the café. Her lips are pursed and I say I'll get her a bread roll if she likes. Everyone else is already there eating bacon rolls like they haven't eaten for a week. The boys have two or three on their plates. Jake looks the happiest I've seen him, ever. Big Ben's sitting with Martin Aston and he looks away when he sees me. This makes me sad. I missed running with him this morning and him timing me to a nanosecond.

'Morning, girls,' says Le Temps.

I jump. I hadn't noticed him. I was expecting Season to come out of the kitchen looking like Season, even though she's become a Carnivore overnight. Maybe when she smiles she'll have fangs instead of teeth. But I wasn't expecting Le Temps.

'Where's Season?' I say.

'Season's off season today,' he says, smiling.

I don't know why he's smiling from East to West. It isn't a very good joke.

'No, she isn't,' I say. 'Her car's outside. What have you done to her? Have you locked her in the pantry?'

'Now, now,' says Le Temps. 'Save your accusations. She came in early but felt unwell. She had to leap home. She was too ill to drive.'

I don't believe him. Season loves her car almost as much as Big Ben does. She wouldn't leave Fiona even if she were vomiting like she was after the party. Ama lowers her eyes at Le Temps but says nothing. Once she realises I'm not going to say anything else, she rises to get her breakfast.

I watch Ama at the serving counter. And, guess who's on the other side, throwing rashers of bacon onto white bread rolls that have been torn rather than cut in half? Mange-Tout! Why are they here? It's supposed to be a robot-free zone. Mange-Tout wasn't on the introductory film. Does Millennia know about this?

I'm hungry but can't eat a thing. Le Temps has broken the rule. The only time you're allowed meat in The Beanstalk is on a leap day, and even then you can only transport it through the café to cook outside. You can't cook and eat it on the premises.

Ama sits down and begins eating her roll bursting with two large rashers, grilled so the fat's gone all crispy.

'You have to eat,' she says, taking a large bite. She pushes a plate in front of me with two white rolls on it. 'Or you'll get sick.'

She sounds like Grandma. I know Ama's being kind but I just can't swallow anything. My stomach's gurgling with hunger but I'm not going to eat. Ama shrugs her shoulders and says something about giving them to Eve. Everything about this day is wrong. I've been looking forward to baking bread ever since I saw Season in the film and now it isn't going to happen.

As if he can read my mind, Le Temps bashes a spoon on a cup and everyone goes quiet, even Jake.

'You will know by now, Season is unwell today so I'm standing in with some assistance. We're low-staffed today.' He nods at Mange-Tout, who smiles the metallic smile, and I remember the announcement that our teachers are spending the day with Millennia on Missing Leapling Alert. MC^2 has the day off but he's working secret solo to find Noon. Maybe Mange-Tout is allowed on the premises to help because you have to have at least two members of staff. That's the rule.

'However, we shall still bake bread. Not in The Beanstalk kitchen but outside.'

There are a few cheers. Even I'm happy to go outside. It's warm and sunny now the fog has lifted, the first day it hasn't rained. Le Temps asks us to go back to our chalets to pack our raincoats in case the weather turns. And our Chronophones. We should reassemble in the café at 9 a.m.

∞

Back in the café, Le Temps announces the second Oops.

'Terribly sorry,' he says, 'but you have to hand in your Chronophones. Millennia's orders.' His mouth turns up at the edges but I don't think he's smiling. There's some chatting and one or two pupils swear, so I can't repeat what they say but I understand they're angry about the Oops. Most of the pupils hand in their phones. I hand in my Chronophone but I know my TwentyTwenty is safe in my bag. Le Temps doesn't know about that. Big Ben and Ama just look at him.

'Why? It's our right to have protection,' says Ama. Her mouth is a dash – and she gives him the bull's-eye.

'Exactly, young lady. There's been a report of cyberbullying so we have to monitor your phones for your PROTECTION.'

'I left mine in the chalet,' says Ama.

I don't believe her but say nothing in case I say the wrong thing and Ama gets angry with me again.

'Then I suggest you go back to the chalet for it.'

His voice sounds like his mouth is too big for the words and they echo in it. Ama grabs her bag and leaves the room. She makes the café door slam behind her and we all jump. I didn't think doors could slam here. I thought they invented them to be quiet. I'm scared Ama's going to get into trouble.

I look at Big Ben. The sun's shining through the window on him like a spotlight. He's muttering under his breath and it's hard to hear what he's saying but I think he might be counting. Le Temps's eyebrows dip into his eyes.

'Ben. Your phone, please.'

Big Ben looks at the ground. Le Temps turns to me.

'Maybe you could persuade Ben to hand over his phone?'

Big Ben stops muttering. It's worse now because I don't know what he's going to do next. Is he going to throw a chair? But he doesn't throw a chair. I think his Anger Management strategies are starting to work. He rummages in his bag, produces his Chronophone and aims it across the room at Le Temps like he's throwing a javelin. Le Temps catches it mid-air. It's a good catch and Jake whoops. I don't know whether he's whooping the throw or the catch or both. Le Temps shakes his head at Big Ben.

Then it's silent. Like the whole café's on pause. No one says a word. Everyone, even Jake, is looking at the floor. Then Big Ben stands up, stays standing like a statue for ages, like he isn't sure what to do with his body. I think he's grown two inches this week alone. And runs out of the room.

He leaves as Ama arrives back, Chronophone in her hand. She doesn't throw it like Big Ben. She hands it in, sucks her teeth like Grandma does when someone tries to charge her too much in the market and walks slowly out of the room with her head in the air. Le Temps shows his teeth like an advert.

'Thank you for your cooperation,' he says.

I'm surprised he doesn't tell her or Big Ben to come back. I'm scared they're both going to get into trouble later today when the teachers and Millennia are back. Le Temps isn't like a normal teacher at all. Maybe because he plans the land, he breaks the rules. I don't know what to do because I'm angry Le Temps humiliated Big Ben, and scared Big Ben and Ama will get into trouble. I want to walk out too and do running but I definitely don't want to get sent home from Leap 2048 for breaking the rules. It would be a disgrace. I hear some buzzing in my bag. I know as soon as I hear the buzzing it must be my TwentyTwenty. What if it's another Predictive? But I can't check it. I have to keep my phone a secret. Especially now.

∞

'Today we shall bake stokbrot, also known as stickbread. Forget yeast. Forget cosy ovens. This is survival food.'

It's fun. I find it hard at first because it isn't exactly what it said on the timetable. But it is still breadmaking and I've been looking forward to it all week. Though Le Temps might be lying about Season, has confiscated our phones and has an assistant robot with metal teeth, and is bad, he IS a good teacher. He helps us make the dough out of all-white ingredients – flour, baking powder, sugar, salt, oil and water – wind it round a stick and cook it on the campfire.

It's the best bread I've ever eaten.

The workshop is so good I forget to check my phone. It would be difficult anyway because when Le Temps isn't looking straight at me, Mange-Tout is. I think it's deliberate. They're watching me all through the workshop, especially when I'm eating the bread. After that, they aren't watching me quite as much and I remember but I don't want to risk it. Maybe it was SOS L. But if it were SOS L, it would be too early. It's still morning. SOS L is supposed to happen at 11 o'clock this evening.

It's only on the way back to the centre once the workshop's over and I manage to get behind the workshop leaders that I'm able to look at my phone deep inside my bag. I don't want to pull it out in case one of the other pupils sees it and tells Le Temps. A message has come up.

Come to chalet after workshop. Delete this. Ama.

∞

Ama, Eve and I are sitting in the chalet. GMT's nowhere to be seen. They've spent all morning talking about Kwesi. When I opened the door, they were sitting cross-legged on the rug, giggling. I felt sad. Maybe Ama was best friends with Eve now. But Ama grabbed my hand immediately and almost dragged me into the room. I didn't complain. This must be her way of saying she likes me.

'We've cracked the code,' she says.

'What code?' I perch on the edge of my bed. 'SOS L?'

'No. SOS L's history.' She rolls her eyes anticlockwise. 'LEAP 2100. Where Kwesi said he was going.'

'It's not a leap year!'

'Exactly. But it's important. Eve says Kwesi mentioned it to them too. Said there was something odd, he was leaping to 2100. He MUST be there!'

'We think darling sis is there too.' Eve rearranges her legs on the rug. I notice she's wearing purple and green leggings with matching trainers. Ama's.

'Elle, if you were leaping to 2100,' says Ama, 'what date would you leap to?'

'The Olympic Games. I don't know the date, they haven't announced it yet!'

Mexico City was the 12th of October because of the climate. I don't say this because Ama's giving me the bull's-eye.

'THINK, Elle,' she says. 'Not Olympics. General. What date would Leaplings leap to?'

'They wouldn't leap.'

'What d'you think, Eve?'

'Haven't the foggiest. Not sure I have the skills. When I leapt here, I almost ended up in 2050.'

Ama shakes her head like a dog shaking off water after a swim, stands up and starts doing pacing.

'Don't they teach you Leaplings anything? How I understand it, you can leap to any date but it's easier to leap on a leap day. Or the equivalent. The 28th of February or the 1st of March.'

'Leap 2100 doesn't exist,' I say. 'So why do you think they're there?'

'For the rendezvous, of course. Or it's a commune.' She sounds like GMT. I wonder where GMT is. She won't be at lunch eating dead animals in bread.

'Are we going to leap there?' I say.

'I can't,' says Ama. 'But you or Eve can.'

I look at Eve and she looks back at me without blinking. 2100 is an anti-leap year so it'll be extra hard to do the trip alone. It could be dangerous. The furthest I've leapt solo is two hours ahead. Neither of us volunteers.

'Shall we talk phones?' says Eve.

'Why? To change the subject?' says Ama. 'You Leaplings do my head in. What's the point in having The Gift if you don't use it?' She sucks her teeth and walks out of the room, slamming the door for the second time today. I feel sad Ama's so angry.

Eve looks at me, takes a deep breath and talks phones. When Ama went back to the chalet this morning, she told Eve we had to hand in our Chronophones. Eve reminded her she still had hers. Le Temps doesn't know about Eve's phone. We can use it for emergencies. They put the Time Squad number and all our contacts onto Eve's phone. So Ama felt better about handing her Chronophone back. We must have a strategy with the phones, now we know my TwentyTwenty's still working. The text this morning came through no problem.

'Elle, let's swap. You have mine. It's off their radar; they don't know the number. I'll camp here with the TwentyTwenty. Any problems, text me.'

I can't imagine Eve camping in the chalet all afternoon. It's a warm day and she's got more energy than all of us put together. Even her words spark with energy. I bet she'll get bored and leap to 2100 and find Kwesi and Noon. And I don't like the idea of swapping phones. Though I haven't used it all week, I want to keep my own phone in my own bag. Eve's Chronophone is silver. I wish it was white. But things are serious now. Kwesi, Noon and Season are missing. If Le Temps is cutting off our communication, what will he do next?

Eve gives me her Chronophone. I take it in my right hand. I'm still holding the TwentyTwenty in my left. She raises her eyebrows. I move my left hand towards her but can't bring myself to let go. My phone = my life. Even though I got trolled in 2020. Even though it can't make calls in the past or the future. The present is 2048. It works in the present. Eve holds out her hand. She smiles at me.

Kwesi, Noon and Season are missing.

I hand over the TwentyTwenty.

My lifeline's in her hands.

Chapter 18:00

SURVIVAL OF THE FITTEST

The afternoon workshop is also held outside. Le Temps says the weather has been kind to us but I don't agree. It's munny – muggy and sunny at the same time – hot as June, not like March at all. The air feels heavy, the sun harsh. The sky is a sickly yellow.

The workshop is running round the grounds, excluding the woods. There's a flat field behind the centre where the Annuals did jumping yesterday when I was taken ill. I think the original plan was to kill animals in the woods but Le Temps is trying to be nice to us. He doesn't want any more arguments. I see him yawning. He must be tired, running two workshops in one day. Thankfully, Mange-Tout isn't there. I hope they've been locked away in a metal cell, where they belong.

Le Temps says my running style is superb but I don't answer him. I'm running with my bag on my back because I'm scared if I put it down my phone will buzz and Le Temps will confiscate it like they do in school if you use your phone unauthorised in lessons. Eve's the kind of girl who sends loads of text messages, especially as no one else can send texts in 1924. She'd do it for light amusement, darling. I hope she doesn't, though. We agreed the phones are for emergency use only.

I notice Big Ben watching me running. I miss him. I hope he wants to run with me again tomorrow. But I don't say anything to him, because if I say the wrong thing he'll go from 0 to 10 and do something bad and get sent home. Ama's also ignoring me. But when I'm running I forget how scared I am when people are angry with me. When I'm running, I get into the zone. My brain stops playing things over and over, like the film for Leap 2048 when Season is kneading the big lump of white dough. Although I play things I like, sometimes I want them to stop but my brain refuses and keeps playing scenes in a loop. When I'm running, I don't even think about Bob Beamon. I don't think at all. I just run.

I'm halfway round the field when we hear it, see it. The sky lights up like a blank screen. A few seconds later, a crack of thunder so loud I jerk mid-stride. Rain like needles. No wind at all. I keep on running. It's actually OK running in the rain. When I was younger, I hated rain and refused to walk to school on wet days. Grandma had to phone the school to get them to collect me in a car. But now it's OK. When it's raining, it's like running in the shower. You don't get so hot and sweaty. If you want, you can lift your head up to the sky and drink it so you don't get dehydrated. I hope future rain is safe to drink. I look up at the sky and open my mouth. A few black spots move slowly overhead.

As I get back to the centre side of the field, I see Le Temps waving at me. I don't wave back. I keep on running. He's broken the spell. I was in the zone and now my brain starts thinking again. Thinking about Kwesi and Noon and Season and GMT and Big Ben and Ama and Le Temps and *Robert Beamon jumps*. Now he's shouting, so I have to think about why he's shouting. Then I realise everyone else has gone in. I'm the only one still outside. Le Temps's tracksuit is totally wet. He looks at me with dead-fish eyes.

'Do you understand the word stop, Elle? What is it with you?'

'I was in the zone.'

'Well, the zone is now the Common Room. If you're not there in two minutes, I'll . . .' He looks up to the sky and blinks against the rain. 'Give you detention.'

'This isn't school, it's Leap 2048,' I say, and his mouth curves up at the edges but I don't think he's happy. He rolls his eyes clockwise.

'Indeed,' he says. 'Indeed.'

I don't like the way he's staring at me like he's laughing at me, so I run inside to the Common Room.

∞

I enjoy watching the storm. It's like a film of a storm when you're inside and can't feel the rain. We're watching it through the big glass windows that look out onto the field. The sheet lightning makes the grass look like cartoon grass, bright with black edges. Then the thunder comes. Then lightning and thunder at the same time. I feel like the storm's in my head. Maria starts crying. I never knew she hated storms. I wish Mrs C Eckler was here to look after her. I'm scared she's going to reach 10 in panic. Le Temps's eyebrows drop to his eyes like rainclouds.

We're all sprawled across seats and beanbags and the big circular rug in the Common Room. GMT's back. Her hair's dry so she must have been indoors somewhere. I wonder where she went. Le Temps has given up trying to teach us anything. But he's not allowed to leave us all on our own. Even he keeps some of the rules.

Even if I tried, I wouldn't be able to hear myself think. Maria's crying louder now. GMT's trying to comfort her with a cuddle but not doing a very good job. Maria says something in Portuguese like she does when she's angry. But this time she's scared. I put my hands over my ears. Her crying's making my heart pound. Le Temps suddenly stands up, rigid as a statue like Big Ben does when he's gone from 0 to 10.

'Shut up! It's only a storm!'

GMT looks angry. 'It's your fault,' she says to Le Temps. Everyone stares. We wouldn't talk to a grown-up like that. But GMT's 4-leap now. That makes her a grown-up.

'My fault, indeed? Who made her weak? Her parents. Should have put her out in a storm as a baby. Look at her now. Pathetic.'

'Not Maria. The storm, man! You think it's cool to eat meat and dump waste. You drowned London, New York, San Francisco. We're all gonna—'

But she doesn't finish her sentence. Le Temps interrupts.

'I may be called Le Temps but I don't play God. Nature does what she likes. Nothing to do with man.'

Everything goes into slow motion. This can't be happening. His words echo in my head and my mind is right back in my 2020 classroom, Pete LMS humiliating me, echoing the words of his dad. This can't be happening. I can't believe it. Le Temps is Pete LMS's dad! My legs and feet have a mind of their own. I'm standing up and speaking before my brain has caught up.

'You're Pete LMS's dad,' I say.

'Who's he when he's at home?' says Le Temps. But unfortunately he isn't at home, in 2020. He's here, in 2048. In this room.

'A factory farmer. His son was a bully. IS a bully,' I say. 'He goes to my school.'

'Indeed,' says Le Temps. 'I'm sure his father wouldn't be happy with that accusation.'

'You're lying,' I say. 'You're Pete LMS's dad. You've hidden Season in a cupboard and cooked meat in her kitchen and disappeared Kwesi and Noon and stolen our phones and you're a witchcraft and I'm going to report you and you're going to get locked up and sent to prison ad infinitum!'

The room goes crazy. I never heard so much whooping. GMT says, 'Far out!', Jake pretends he's had his head chopped off, Ama raises her fist in the air and Big Ben leaps across the room and high-fives me. When I sit down, I'm shaking, angry and happy at the same time. I'm not scared any more. I don't care if I'm sent home. I don't care if I'm excluded from the trip. Le Temps is bad to the power of 3. Enough is enough.

'Bravo, Elle!' he says. 'There's the spirit. Knew you had it in you. Worthy of an Oscar, at least.'

I don't know whether anyone heard him because they're making too much noise. Why is he praising me? I thought he was going to give me detention. His face is red and I can smell his sweat from across the room. His voice is his normal buttery voice but his body is the opposite. His body is angry and scared at the same time. I want to look at him and I don't want to look at him. I want to see what his body does next, whether his words match it, but I hate looking at him because he's a criminal. Not a criminal like MC^2 who stole watches and didn't kill no one. A REAL criminal.

Beneath the chaos in the Common Room, voices in the corridor outside. With the rain and the whooping, we were distracted. The teachers are back. Even when they open the door the noise continues. No one tries to stop, they've gone too far into chaos. Mrs C Eckler stands in the corner of the room with her mouth a capital O; Mr C Eckler has a minus mouth. Millennia marches into the centre of the room and raises both arms like she's going to take flight. Then I realise her hands are flat like she's pushing a heavy object. The heavy object is the sound we're making. She doesn't shout like the Head at Intercalary International. She doesn't need to. When Millennia freezes her hands, her eyes focused on each and every one of us, everyone stops shouting.

∞ Chapter 19:00 ∞

0 TO 60 IN 1.4 SECONDS

Millennia doesn't send us home. She speaks to us in the room without Le Temps and asks us questions about what happened. I can't go into details in front of everybody. I'm already worried Ama will be cross I mentioned Kwesi and Noon. Millennia talks with us for a long time. I don't listen to it all until I hear her voice change, like she's talking to adults rather than children.

'Le Temps is a trusted colleague, an exceptional eco-landscaper. He has won awards. Yes, he is a little unconventional, but that is a mark of his genius.' She smiles at all of us. 'You are welcome to make an appointment to see me, individually, in my office, Y2K. I am free tomorrow morning.

'Please accept my apologies for the change of plans brought about by Season's absence. Season texted me personally to say she needed time-out. She will be back tomorrow.'

I'm pleased to hear that. Even adults need time-out. Le Temps hasn't locked Season in a cupboard. I wrongly accused him of that. Millennia doesn't want to disrupt the itinerary any more than it has been. Dinner and the evening's activity will proceed according to timetable. This evening we have free time.

∞

We're all quiet at dinner. The afternoon's worn us out. One good thing: Big Ben's talking to me again! He's sitting next to me wearing the red hat. Ama's on the other side and GMT opposite. Everything feels normal. Except Kwesi and Noon are still missing, Season's off and Le Temps is King of the Kitchen.

Tonight, he's kept to Season's colour-coded menu. Mange-Tout is nowhere to be seen. But when I go up to the counter, Le Temps winks at me.

'You could have mashed potato and tofu. Or fish pepper soup with yam. Your choice.'

I narrow my eyes. Why is he being nice to me when I was nasty to him?

'There aren't any fish in 2048. That's an Anachronism!'

He smiles. 'Still feisty as ever. You're perfect, Elle. Quite perfect. But, swear on my father's life, I found mackerel in the freezer labelled 2022. 26 years old! Not smuggled. Neglected. A little frost-bitten but . . .' He shrugs his shoulders. 'Up to you.'

I wish it didn't smell so good. My mouth is already full of saliva. Mackerel is oily rather than white fish but I could eat with my eyes closed. Le Temps may be a bad man but he's a good cook. Season said no meat was allowed in her kitchen. She didn't mention fish. Le Temps pushes the bowl towards me and the aroma is too tempting. He puts another bowl on the tray with three small pieces of yam and some coconut oil. How did he know that was my favourite dish? Even though it's dinner, not breakfast, I walk back to our table and put down the bowl. Ama's eyes go bigger than Jupiter.

'Fish! How on earth . . .'

'Le Temps found mackerel in the freezer,' I say.

'And you believed him?'

'He might be telling the truth. He didn't lock Season in a cupboard.'

'Doesn't mean he's innocent.' Ama shakes her head. I can see she wants to eat the fish pepper soup. Pepper soup is popular in Ghana too. Even Big Ben's interested. He loves spicy food. He leans over it, breathes in, breathes out.

'Elle, he isn't Pete LMS's dad. The maths is wrong. Pete LMS's dad is old now.'

'What?'

'He's old in 2020. My mum knows him. Why did you say—'

'When Pete LMS was bullying me, he said his DAD said, "Nature does what she likes. Nothing to do with man."'

Ama laughs.

'Elle, lots of people say the same things. Doesn't make them the same PERSON.' Then she turns to my soup again. 'You're not going to eat it, are you?'

I don't know whether Ama thinks I SHOULDN'T eat it or that I'm not going to eat it. Maybe she wants to eat it instead. I do want the soup. It's the best pepper soup I've ever smelled. But I remember MC^2 making sure the sweets were sweet. Maybe the soup's been drugged. Before I can make up my mind what to do, Big Ben takes a giant spoonful and coughs so much I have to hit him on the back. His face has gone purple. He's still coughing and I'm still thumping when the rest of the room goes quiet. I think everyone's watching me and Big Ben but then I see they're looking towards the door.

Eve has walked into the room.

She's still wearing the purple and green leggings but she's changed into GMT's platforms so it's an odd match. For a second, she pauses, looking around, then walks across to our table. People start talking again. They think she's Noon. She sits down beside Ama.

'Sorry,' she says, 'about this morning. Forgive me, darling?' She pauses again, then says, to all of us, 'Couldn't lie low. I was STARVING.'

I watch her walk up to the counter and Le Temps freezes like when he shouted at Maria but he doesn't look angry, he looks scared. Why is he so scared of Eve? Does he think she's Noon or has he worked out she's a twin? Maybe he's scared of twins. In Nigeria, in the olden days, people used to starve twins because they thought they were witchcrafts. He only freezes for a split second. Then he looks normal again. Eve doesn't seem to notice. She carries her food back on a tray and eats like she hasn't eaten in a week. Which is probably true. I feel bad I forgot to take more food back at lunchtime. Of course, she missed the wonderful bread workshop.

'Elle, are you going to eat that soup or what?' says Ama.

'It might be poisoned.'

'Big Ben's alive.'

I look at him. His face is normal again. I don't think he wants to try any more soup. Ama licks her lips.

'Because if you don't want it, I DO.'

∞

Ama, GMT, Eve, Big Ben and I have taken over the Common Room, sitting on sofas and beanbags. Ama set an Emergency Meeting for 8 p.m. We need to decide who's going to leap to 2100. She's obsessed with it. She and Eve spent an hour doing small talk in the chalet before the meeting. I reread Bob Beamon because I don't do small talk. I like to talk about BIG things.

But when Ama opens the meeting, Eve volunteers immediately. Maybe they weren't doing small talk for an hour after all. Maybe they were plotting.

'Leaping's not my forte, darlings, but I just leapt over a century. Solo. And . . .'

Big Ben's staring at her. His eyebrows almost meet in the middle. 'You've changed,' he says.

Eve laughs. 'You're 36 hours behind, Big Ben. I'm Eve. Noon's twin sister. Noon's missing. We think she might be with Kwesi.'

Big Ben freezes for a few seconds and then says, 'There's TWO of you.'

'Yes. Identical only in looks. I'm the noisy one.'

It takes Big Ben a few seconds to smile. What a relief. I thought he might struggle with meeting someone new. But maybe it's

OK because the new person looks identical to the person he already knows. Maybe he finds it exciting to meet an identical twin.

Ama's shuffling around in her seat. 'Guys,' she says. 'Focus! Anyone else volunteer to leap?'

'What date and time and place?' says Big Ben.

'The 28th of Feb. Or the 1st of March. We couldn't agree on a time.' She pauses. 'And never discussed place.'

'Place is important,' I say. 'If you leap without focus you could end up in Brazil. That would be stupid.' I thought of Brazil because we studied the destruction of the Amazon Rainforest in geography. Everyone looks at me, then looks away. They've all learnt I don't like people staring at me.

'They must be HERE,' says Ama. 'Otherwise why would Kwesi text Leap 2100, like it was a trip. But WHERE here?'

'How about The Round? MC^2 said "leap in The Round an' you'll never be seasick". I saw the Infinity signs.'

'Elle, spill the beans,' says Ama. 'No more secrets.'

It wasn't a secret. There's been so much happening, I forgot. I tell them about MC^2's infinity tattoo and the extra ∞ signs appearing on the trees.

'MC must'a put them there!' It's GMT speaking for the first time. I thought she'd fallen asleep. She's taken her shoes off and stretched out on the sofa. Her nails are painted sparkly silver. '"Once upon a time, a boy wrote a message on a tree." His story.'

Ama sighs. Maybe she's as tired as GMT.

'OK. The Round is significant. Any more volunteers?'

'Me!' Big Ben and I say at the same time. We look at each other. I speak first.

'I was scared before but I leapt yesterday and I still have some sweets so I can eat one if I vomit.'

'No,' says Big Ben. 'I'm a boy. Boys are stronger than girls. I should do it.'

'WHAT?' I say. Big Ben doesn't usually say things like that. He knows I can run faster than boys. But that's not the point.

'It's not about strength,' I say. 'It's ACCURACY. I'm good at concentrating . . .'

'Like yesterday?' says Ama.

'I couldn't see you,' says Big Ben quietly.

'Elle, I know I wanted you to leap this morning but . . . I think it's best you don't.' Ama's scrunching up her forehead. 'If you pass out, there's no one to help you.' She stands up now and begins her pacing. If she put the energy into running she puts into pacing, she'd be talented. 'I think Eve should do it. She's the oldest.'

'That's irrelevant!' I say. I didn't realise it but my voice has got louder. 'Age doesn't matter. Not in 2048.'

'Only old people say that, to feel good. Age might matter in 2100. It's a glitch year. Eve's leapt a century. Alone. Best she does it.'

'I can leap with Eve,' says Big Ben.

'We can't risk TWO going missing,' says Ama.

'Not logical.' Big Ben gets up off his seat.

'We don't have to obey you.' I stare at Ama. 'You're not a teacher.'

Ama gave us a choice, then took it away from us. Which is like lying.

'You guys crack me up,' says GMT. 'MC's on the case. Since this morning.'

Everyone looks surprised except me. I knew he was on a solo mission.

'Meaning what, exactly?' says Ama.

'Leap 2100. He's there! Well, he's not responding to texts but that's what he—'

Ama stops pacing. 'Why didn't you say so earlier?'

'It was kinda entertaining listening to you guys work things out, but . . .' She stretches her legs and reveals her infinity tattoo. 'Some of us got work to do.' She sits up and puts on her Adidas trainers, laces them up.

'So long!' she says and disappears into thin air.

'Typical!' says Ama. 'It's all about HER. What about Kwesi?'

'MC² will find him,' I say. 'He's an Infinite. He'll save Kwesi AND the planet.'

'Thought you said he was a crim?'

'He is, but I like him now. He's no more a criminal than my cat.'

I enjoy the feel of other people's words on my tongue, like Eve tried on GMT's shoes. Eve is sprawled on the sofa like GMT was, with her shoes off, and I notice her toenails are painted with sparkly silver nail polish too. Everyone's trying to be someone else.

But Big Ben has stood up. I know by the way he stood up that he hasn't just gone from 0 to 10. He's gone from 0 to 60. In less than two seconds!

I don't want him to throw a chair and get sent home in disgrace from Leap 2048. I ask if he wants to do running, but he ignores me. I think he's counting in his head. Big Ben can count to 100 in 10 seconds. When he can't sleep, he counts to a million. He looks like he's counting to a million now. Then he abruptly stops counting, grabs each arm of the armchair and I think, please don't throw the armchair, please don't. But he's using the armchair to keep himself still because he's shaking so much, like he's cold. He's shaking so much that when he rushes out of the room he can barely walk, like he can't quite keep control of his body. A few moments later we hear the front door slam and the whoosh of an engine.

Big Ben's hacked into Fiona!

∞

It doesn't take long for everyone to know Big Ben's stolen Fiona. The whole centre's in chaos. Millennia's gone home and the Leapling teachers are making calls on their Chronophones to Season, Millennia, MC^2. They can't call the police. How could they answer detailed questions without breaking the Oath? The Annual teachers are trying to calm us all down. Some of the pupils, like Jake, think it's amazing Big Ben worked out how to steal the car but others, even Martin Aston, are scared Big Ben's going to have a crash and die. We all know he can drive but he's never driven a Ferrari Forever before.

I want to live under the table. I know I upset Big Ben but I don't understand why he got angry. To make things worse, Ama and Eve are best friends now and ignoring me because they think it's my fault. Even Mrs C Eckler is too busy to help me. I want to live under the table but I can't live under the table because the Common Room is bursting with pupils. Most of the teachers are in the hall, where they can make calls with less background noise. I think about going back to the chalet but I want to hear if they find Big Ben. I want to be the first to hear. I must remain in the centre.

I'm walking along the lower ground floor corridor. It's quiet here. I've never walked down here before. We've only ever been in the hall or The Igloo. This must be where Millennia's office is: **Y2K**. It says her name in bold black capital letters underneath. Next to that, another door: **Energy Equals: MC^2**. Opposite **The Hourglass: SEASON**. Next to it: **The Time Machine: LE TEMPS**.

All of a sudden I get that funny feeling. It reminds me of something and it almost comes into my head, then escapes again. I concentrate on the writing, hoping it will come back but it doesn't. Footsteps along the hall. I turn around to see Le Temps. He's still dressed in his tracksuit from earlier, still smelling of sweat.

'Terribly sorry about your boyfriend, Elle.'

'He's not my boyfriend. Why are YOU sorry? Did you make him steal the car?'

Nigerians say they're sorry when they've done nothing wrong. They say sorry to show that they feel sad like you do. But Le Temps isn't Nigerian. He's English pretending to be French, with his clever-clever name.

'No. He stole it of his own free will. I'm sorry he made a wrong decision. Still,' he smiles, 'better than rearranging the furniture.'

As Le Temps is speaking, I'm reading his name on his office door like the words have come up as the caption 'LE TEMPS, Eco-landscaper' and Le Temps is a talking head. And there's something about the order. Something familiar. I play the film over in my head and I focus in on the words 'LE TEMPS' on the screen. Then I look back at **LE TEMPS** on the door. And I focus again on the film, rewind to the letters flying all over the screen like insects and I look back at the letters on the door, focus until the letters leap out of place: **LETEMPS**, **LTMSEEP**, **LSM PTEE**, the letters rearrange and rearrange until they stop. **PETE LMS**. Le Temps is an anagram of Pete LMS.

Le Temps = Pete LMS.

Chapter 20:00

THE PREDICTIVE

'You're Pete LMS grown up!'

'Bravo, Elle. Pure genius.' He clicks his Chronophone, his office door opens and he guides me inside. 'After you. Was wondering when you'd work that out.'

His office is as large as our flat. It has a desk with a green computer on it, two comfy armchairs and a round rug based on an old-fashioned clock with roman numerals. On the wall is a large whiteboard with strings of letters on it, like someone fell onto a keyboard, and various dates, all of them leap years in the mid-21st century. And 2100.

'Welcome to The Time Machine. Do take a seat. D'you think I did a good job on the anagram? Reinventing myself. We Annuals like wordplay too, you know. Ah, you thought I was a Leapling. The name fools everyone. Can't leap to save my life. You won't tell on me, will you? Our little secret?'

He sits down in one of the armchairs but I don't sit down. I stand near the door, staring at him in his tracksuit with his bald head. He looks nothing like his younger self. I can't believe Le Temps is Pete LMS. But he is. He is.

'What are YOU doing here?'

'You named me, Elle. Remember? Second Year. Nickname stuck for a decade. You never liked anything I posted on Facebook. Other people's, never mine. Called me Pete LMS behind my back. But eventually I got used to it, as one does. Liked it, even. Letters after my name gave me a certain . . . gravitas. Even teachers used it eventually. But what I really wanted, Elle,' he taps into his Chronophone, 'was for you to like ME.'

'You're lying.'

'You may find this hard to believe, my dear, but it's true.'

'Then why did you humiliate me all the time?'

'I liked you but I was jealous. You were clever and sporty and Big Ben was a maths genius. The whole class had lessons I wasn't allowed into. I never fitted in. I was a nobody.'

'You were a bully!'

'Terribly sorry. Misspent youth and all that. But you can't change the past.'

'You're lying. You could send your 2020 self a message on your Chronophone. STOP BULLYING NOW.'

'I COULD,' he says, 'but I don't think that's necessary, Elle. You can stand up for yourself now, without my help.'

He taps into his phone again. He hasn't changed at all. Still obsessed with technology. Still bad.

'What have you done with Kwesi and Noon?'

'Not guilty. You Leapers excel at disappearing acts. First one I saw was outside a certain geography classroom . . .'

My mouth forms a capital O. 'You saw me—'

'Excellent, Elle. Yes. It was supposed to be a punishment. Stand outside the classroom, repent. Instead, a veritable treat. I saw you disappear into the ether. Took me a decade to find out about The Gift. Of course, I told no one. Knowledge is power. Very few of us know.' He gestures to one of the armchairs. 'Do take a seat, you're making me nervous.'

'What have you done?'

'Kwesi, yes. Very bright, nonverbal, good at the long jump if I remember correctly. And his paintwork, marvellous, just marvellous.'

'His PB was 5 metres 90, which is an 89.49% age grade. But he specialised in the triple jump.'

'Indeed. And Moon, yes. Not so bright but more sparkly. Leaps like lightning!'

'Her name's Noon, not Moon. It's a palindrome. What do you mean, sparkly?'

'Never realised she had a twin. Threw me for a second. Two stupid names rather than one.'

'That's not true. You don't even know them. They're worth four of you!'

I look at the door. Why didn't I just run away before he guided me in? Why don't I leap to safety now? Because I'd never find out what SOS L means. The clue must be somewhere in this office.

'Elle, how would you like to go to the Music, Maths and

Movement School? They have the best athletics facilities in the country.'

'I can't. I already go to Intercalary International.'

'The Triple M would suit you. But the Double M would reward you.'

'The Double M?'

'My boss, Millennia. Known in our circle as MM. The mastermind. She gives the orders. You could go to school in the week and have a weekend job here.'

'In 2048?'

'No. In 2100. I've established a business in the future.'

'2100?' I narrow my eyes.

'Seriously, Elle. I see your talent. Come and work for me.'

'Doing what?'

'I make more money than you could ever imagine. You wouldn't have to live in a pokey little flat. You could live in a mansion, have your own training facilities.' He's still tapping his phone. I look around the office, at the whiteboard covered in letters and dates.

'Have you been to our flat?'

'No. But I can imagine it.' He gives me the bull's-eye. I look away. 'What do you say?'

'What's the job?'

'Assisting my undertaking?'

'Funerals?' I don't want to work with dead bodies. They would rot and smell and make me sick.

'Not exactly. Freudian slip. Shall we say, I supply the demand.'

'For what?'

'Meat.' He gets up from his chair and turns on the computer. It makes a whirring sound as the screen lights up. 'Since the Rations, I've made millions.'

'You're a smuggler?'

'No, no. My Old Leapers do all that. They can leap. I can't. They luggaged me to set it all up but now I leave it to the ancients and the robots.'

'That's an Anachronism and it's illegal and you should all go to prison.'

'It's a bit naughty, yes. But people will always eat meat. Mange-Tout coined the slogan MAN=BEAST. The Vegetables still quote it. Equal rights for animals and people, they say.'

'That's not true. MAN=BEAST doesn't mean PEOPLE, it doesn't mean men. It just means one man. You. You're an animal!' I take a slow step back towards the door.

'No, Elle. It's not about me. The slogan's a bit old, I give you that. But it gave me the idea. MAN=BEAST. What about a man-beast hybrid? Meat was rotting in transit, the animals' bodies couldn't withstand the leap. We needed a magic ingredient to preserve it. I thought human DNA . . .'

'People! You eat people! You're a . . . a . . . cannibal!' This is worse than I imagined. It's not like Le Temps is stuck on a desert island with no other food to eat, and even then he should cut off his own leg and eat himself first before thinking of eating another human.

He rolls his eyes clockwise. 'I would put it a little more elegantly, if you let me finish. Annual and most Leapling DNA didn't work. But GIFTED Leapers . . . it worked like magic. Simple gene editing. We did a cut-and-paste with the sheep gene and the Leap gene and came up with a winner. What do you think we called it, Elle?'

I shrug my shoulders. 'Sheepling?'

Le Temps smiles, moves his finger like he's writing the word in the air.

I try again. 'Shleep?'

'Close. You're a natural.' He pauses a few seconds. 'We called it sheap. With an "e" and an "a".'

He raises his eyebrows, like he expects me to speak. I stare back at him until he taps something into his computer and faces me again.

'Thought you might appreciate the wordplay, Elle. It's our bestselling product on the Black Market. It's eaten by people all over the world. Those who can afford it.'

'I only eat white food, so I'd never eat it.'

'I'm not asking you to EAT it. But you'd make us a fortune in marketing. Or you could run the factory. Your choice. Of course, sheap's the code, not the brand name. The public never need know.'

And it's then I remember the leap day barbecue, the guessing game. We couldn't guess the mystery meat because it was a new invention. That explains why Le Temps gave Big Ben the bull's-eye when he guessed sheep.

'The barbecue . . .'

'Clever girl. Ben nearly guessed on the night. There's only a subtle difference in taste. We use DNA from young truants, if you're wondering. Leap criminals. I treat them better than they deserve. Give them work, food, clothing.'

'Criminals? YOU'RE the criminal. You're a monster!'

Kwesi. Noon. Too many Leaps gone missing.

'I wouldn't put it quite like that.'

'The devil incarnate.'

'I prefer Carnivore.' He sits down at the computer, logs in and swivels his office chair around. 'Work for me, Elle. You'd have a top salary, all the white meat and fish you could eat.'

'I'd rather projectile vomit,' I say and move towards the door.

Le Temps clicks his phone. The door won't open. He makes a sad face.

'Elle Bíbi-Imbelé, you're so clever, you're stupid. Do you know what's REALLY clever? Surviving when you haven't got The Gift. Having to work till your hands bleed. Making money. That's life, Elle! And you, with The Gift and the brains, refuse the chance of a better life.'

'Better for you, not for me. Let me out!'

'To tell everyone my business? I don't think so. But I'm enjoying our little chat. Very much.'

I must leap out of here. But I have to close my eyes to concentrate and he'll know what I'm doing and stop me. And I need to message Eve, so she knows Le Temps is a criminal. I must get help. I must find a way to distract him.

'Are you still on Facebook?' I say.

'No. It died a death. I set up my own website to recruit staff. Modelled on Facebook.' He swivels his chair and starts tapping.

His page comes up and he logs in. As I unzip my bag, he swivels back to face me.

'I use a different name, of course. And no photo. I'm too well-known.'

I remember Millennia saying he's won awards.

'Do you have conversations with people?'

'All the time. Look!'

He's facing the screen. I quietly take the phone out of my bag.

'That's lots of conversations,' I say. I tap on the messages icon. I know what I must do.

'Yes. I have hundreds of Friends . . .' He's scrolling down his Friends list.

I tap the caps lock on the phone . . .

'3,274, to be exact.'

. . . and I do what I must do. I type:

'SOS L . . .'

. . . and in the same moment, Le Temps swivels his chair back.

'What are you doing, Elle?'

I press send and the phone makes a whooshing noise and SOS L is sent to my TwentyTwenty and I'm shaking. I wanted to type 'SOS LE TEMPS LOCKED ME IN HIS OFFICE. DEFINITELY A CRIMINAL' so Eve could get help but there wasn't time. I should have sent it to 2000 so the Time Squad could come and arrest Le Temps. I can't do that now.

The phone says 23:00.

Predictives don't lie.

Le Temps leaps out of his chair, snatches the phone from my hand.

'SOS L,' he says, in his voice. 'A message to your Leaper boyfriend?'

He throws my phone across the room. It crashes on the floor and the back comes off. I have to concentrate to pick it up, my hand is shaking so much.

'He's my BEST friend.'

I must keep talking to distract Le Temps. But if I'm talking I can't concentrate to leap. To be safe, I must leap forward in time AND place. The only time I can think of is Leap 2100. MC^2 and GMT must be there. They can help me. I must keep talking. If I talk about something I know well, it will keep me calm. Then I might be able to concentrate at the same time.

'My favourite Olympics is 1968 when Bob Beamon made a world record in the long jump of 8.90 metres. *Robert Beamon jumps and makes sports history. The makers of the measuring instrument never foresaw a jump so staggering.* Mr Branch says it was the most political of Olympics since 1936, when Jesse Owens got four gold medals and made Hitler leave the stadium. In 1968, Tommie Smith and John Carlos did the Black Power salute wearing black gloves on the medal podium and got suspended from the US team. Dick Fosbury raised his fist during his medal ceremony in solidarity with Black Power. Dick Fosbury was white and he invented a new way of doing the high jump called the Fosbury Flop,' I say.

'You really HAVE found your voice, Elle. Some speech. Pity I have to silence you.'

When he emphasises the word silence, I lose my concentration. He takes one step towards me. He holds up his Chronophone like his gun when he shot the rabbit that was a hare. And I know what he wants to do.

He's going to shoot me.

Concentrate.

'Someone will hear the shot.'

'I have a silencer. And I'm going to silence you. When you wake up, you'll see sense.'

Out of the corner of my eye, I see it. A flicker, a split-second outline of a body, a boy, a boy with clumps of hair coming out of his head like antennae, pointing a Chronophone at Le Temps. Before the outline is filled in, it says, in the voice of MC^2:

'Le Temps. Drop the phone. You're under arrest.'

∞

MC^2 is pointing his Chronophone at Le Temps.

Millennia and Season appear from thin air.

Le Temps drops his phone onto the floor.

'What in the name of Time is going on?' says Millennia.

Her hair looks less spiky, like she's just got out of bed. But she's not wearing pyjamas or even a dressing-gown. She's wearing her usual purple hooded cloak. Season looks like she's still IN bed. Her hair's all over the place, she's wearing pyjamas with cars on them and her face is pale. MC^2 blinks his whole body to the other side of the room, still holding his Chronophone.

'Season, rest up. I can handle this. Text GMT.'

'You will do nothing of the sort,' says Millennia, 'until someone explains this SOS.'

'He tried to kill me because I wouldn't work in his factory in 2100 where he mixes Leaplings with sheep to make sheap and sells the meat to people all over the world.'

'Who tried to kill you? Mr E?'

'NO. Le Temps. I mean, Mr T. With his Chronophone!'

'Nonsense, Elle. Chronophones are not guns. Your imagination is quite remarkable. Mr E tells me you have a unique talent for storytelling. Do not confuse fact with fiction.'

I want to tell her it's not a story, it's all true, and I'm remembering she's the Double M big boss pretending to be a centre director and I'm wondering, if Chronophones aren't guns, why is MC^2 still pointing his Chronophone at Le Temps, and appearing, disappearing, appearing all over the room like there's ten of him? There are so many thoughts in my head I want to say all at once, and I feel angry and sad at the same time so I don't say anything at all. Millennia turns to MC^2.

'Mr E, please refrain from your body-popping, lower your Chronophone and explain yourself.'

MC^2 stays in one place but doesn't lower his phone. 'Mr T threatened to silence Elle. He was going to stun her.'

Millennia throws back her head and laughs. It sounds like she's choking on pepper soup.

'It seems,' she says, 'you Leapers have a penchant for fiction. We only have the girl's word and we all know how creative she is with words.'

'Wrong,' says MC^2. 'I clocked the word and the deed.'

I see a brief outline and GMT appears in the room. Season

speaks for the first time. 'We must follow protocol, Miss M. We must call the—'

'Nobody is calling anyone.' Millennia shakes her head like there's a fly inside it. 'There has obviously been a mistake. We all know Mr T has an unusual sense of humour. I'm sure he can explain.'

'Yes. Was hoping I'd be allowed to get a word in,' says Le Temps in his buttery voice. 'Sorry for winding you up, Elle. Got a bit carried away with the drama. One porky pie led to another.'

I find my voice again. 'That's not true! You were going to kill me like the rabbit that was a hare and you're going to prison and all your sheap will leap from their pens so they can't get made into meat.'

Season has taken her phone out of her bag and is tapping the screen. Millennia doesn't notice because she's staring at Le Temps like he's her husband. She's staring so hard it takes her longer than all of us to see the two black hooded figures suddenly appear either side of Le Temps. They must be at least 7 feet tall. I look at them with what-big-eyes but I can't see their eyes at all. Maybe they don't have eyes. Maybe they're robots, like Mange-Tout. MC^2 finally lowers his Chronophone and hands Le Temps's phone to one of the figures.

'Tell 'em the truth, Elle,' he says.

I take a deep breath: 'He threatened to silence me with his Chronophone and disappeared Leaplings to work for him and stole their DNA to edit a sheep into a sheap so he could smuggle it on the Black Market to sell meat to those who can afford it!'

While I'm speaking, the hooded figures hold hands with Le Temps in the middle. He smiles but looks angry and his voice doesn't sound buttery any more.

'The perfect sentence,' he says.

The hooded figures nod and freeze. I know what's going to happen. They're going to leap and Le Temps will leap with them like luggage because he's an Annual. I've heard of Annuals being time-travelled before but never seen it. The moment before they leap, Le Temps winks at Millennia.

'Au revoir, old girl!'

He does it so quickly I almost don't see it. But I do. You only wink at someone you're in love with, so Le Temps must be in love with Millennia like she's in love with him.

Then the hooded giants face each other and squeeze hands and the three of them disappear into thin air.

'I hope he gets ad infinitum,' I say.

Millennia stares at me so long I turn my head to one side.

'Innocent until proven guilty. Many things have changed since 2020 – laws, sentences, prisons – but not the foundations of our legal system.'

'He's a criminal.'

'He's a GENIUS!'

Millennia no longer sounds like Millennia. She's the Double M, 0 to 10 in one second, her hands are shaking and her face looks about to fracture into a thousand pieces. Le Temps was her specialist subject.

'He was, and IS, a trusted colleague. But YOU and Mrs S,' she looks at MC^2, 'have betrayed me. You'll pay for this.' She pauses and fixes me with her cat's-eye, then goes into loudspeaker mode.

'Elle Bíbi-Imbelé Ifíè,' she pronounces my name perfectly, like she can speak Izon, 'again you have thwarted me. You have destroyed a CENTURY of work. And if it takes me every second of a century, I will destroy YOU.'

∞ Chapter 21:00 ∞

2100

I open my eyes. At first, I think I'm in heaven because everything's shiny and white. Maybe Millennia tracked our leap and killed me when we supercharged or everyone dies when they leap to 2100. But a second later I know I'm alive. We're still in Le Temps's office but it's much, much bigger, the size of our assembly hall at school. And it looks like a chemistry lab with white tables and everything made of glass. There's nothing on the tables, though; it's like the scientists cleared everything away and went on holiday. The overhead lights are so dazzling I want to be sick but maybe that's just the leap. At least they don't hum like the ones at school. I try not to move my head. MC^2 and GMT loosen their grip.

'You OK, honeybee?' GMT hands me a sweet. Strawberry. But it's then I realise it isn't the leap that's made me feel sick. It was Millennia shouting at me. Her words are still clanging in my head. The sound AND the sense.

'Leaps, you'll never guess—' MC^2 checks his Chronophone.

'I don't want to guess,' I say. 'Le Temps made me guess the name of his cannibal meat.'

'28 Feb 2100,' says MC^2 and raises his eyebrows at me. 'Elle, I know it was you. How d'ya do it?'

'I tried to think of the 1st of March but Ama said the 28th of February was closer to a leap day on a non-leap year so my brain couldn't help it.'

GMT smiles. 'You outthought us, man. Like you leapt solo. When I tried, couldn't get past '99. MC leapfrogged all the way back to 1860 an' his phone died. You got The Gift in daisy chains.'

I smile. I didn't know I had such a strong Gift. Maybe it's all my athletics training. Big Ben and I train harder than anyone else in the club. I wish he was here now. I suddenly feel sad. So much happened after he left, I forgot he's a missing Leapling too. Where is he?

'What time is it?' I'm trying not to think about missing Big Ben or Millennia's threat. MC^2 shrugs his shoulders.

'Don't know. Signal's gone. Place smells of number two.'

'What's that noise?'

In the far corner of the room is a cage. I don't want to look in the cage in case there's a man-beast hybrid in it with the body of a sheep and the face of a Leapling or vice versa. But MC^2 is already there.

'Just a sheep,' he says.

I look at it out of the corner of my eye. It has a black face and white woolly coat. And it certainly LOOKS like a sheep and SOUNDS like a sheep. But it isn't just a sheep. It can't be.

'Le Temps did a cut-and-paste with the sheep gene and the Leap gene and came up with a winner,' I say.

This must be the sheap with an 'e' and an 'a'. But it doesn't look like it would win prizes. The sheap has pooed all over the floor. But it's not its fault. It would rather be living in fields, not in a chemistry lab. I'm so glad the sheap is alive and not made into burgers and sold to those who can afford it.

We follow the Exit arrow upstairs that reminds me of the ones I came down in 2048 before I reached Le Temps's office. As we get upstairs there's bright daylight. Must be around lunchtime, when the sun comes round. The hall is the same as when we arrived at the centre and Millennia gave her opening address but there are screens all over the walls and the floor's made of glass. MC^2 blinks, tenses his body like he's about to do the run-up to the long jump, but instead of disappearing, appearing, he doesn't move.

'Glitch! We'll have to do this old skool. Room by room in case of guards. Leaps must be locked up someplace. GMT, check outdoors. We'll do inside.'

It's too quiet, like the place has been abandoned, and I wonder if we got the year wrong and we should be sometime else, like 2072. Maybe it's a trap. Maybe Le Temps lied when he said work for me in 2100. MC^2 walks down the white corridor, holding his Chronophone in front of him. Le Temps must have guards working here so people can't come in the middle of the night and steal his prize sheap. All the rooms are empty. I keep thinking I hear noises but I can't work out where they're coming from.

'Did Le Temps kill the Leaplings and bury—?'

GMT bursts into the centre like a firework.

'Guys!' she says. 'Quick! There's a lime-green car circling overhead!'

∞

It's a crash landing! Big Ben's a great driver but he's never flown a Ferrari in driverless mode. He lands in the wood, in the car, eyes closed. Fiona looks like someone's given her a very strong hug. We all sprint over. I get there first. I look at him out of the corner of my eye in case there's blood. I hope the flash of red I'm seeing is only the red hat. What if he's dead? It would be all my fault if he was dead and had killed Fiona.

MC^2 forces the door open and shakes Big Ben's shoulders until GMT gives him the bull's-eye. Big Ben's eyes flick open. It takes him a second to realise it's MC^2 staring into his face, to go from 0 to 10, then he punches him and MC^2 falls back onto the grass like he's done the Fosbury Flop.

'Big Ben,' I say, 'if you hit MC^2 again you'll get excluded from Leap 2048 and sent back to 2020 in disgrace.'

Big Ben gives me the glass-eye, jumps out of the car and hits MC^2 again. MC^2 tries to disappear but it doesn't work. He holds up both hands.

'I ain't fightin' you, bro. We gotta stick tight and save the Leaps.'

Big Ben faces him. 'Are you her boyfriend? Youareyouare youareyouareyouare!'

I wonder if he has concussion from the car crash. You get concussion if you bang your head and it makes you talk nonsense. What's Big Ben talking about? MC^2 sits cross-legged on the ground and blinks.

'Listen, man. She's NOT my girl.'

'Who?' I say.

'YOU, Elle. Man's got it bad. The lovebug. Man needed to flex his biceps, show he's vex. But man saw sense.'

And then I get it, like the answer to a crossword puzzle. I knew Big Ben liked me but didn't realise that's why he got so upset when I said anything nice about MC^2.

'So glad you're OK,' I say. 'And guess what? We haven't found Kwesi or Noon but we found the prize sheap.'

∞

Big Ben isn't impressed with the sheap. I think he wanted it to have two heads or the head of a Leapling and the body of a boy or vice versa. It stinks like a normal sheep.

'It can think aloud, though,' I say and Big Ben scrunches up his eyebrows.

'Not logical.'

'Listen! I can hear it muttering but it isn't opening its mouth.'

'Honeybee, it can't—' GMT does what-big-eyes. 'That's not the sheap. That's voices!'

Everyone goes quiet. There are definitely voices. But where

are they coming from? Has someone come into the building? No. The murmuring is under our feet. But how are we supposed to get underground? The only door is the one with the arrow leading upstairs. MC² is already there.

'Never was no Minus 2, unless . . .' He looks to his right. On the door frame there's a metal code lock. 'Millennia was old skool with tech.' He taps into it.

'Spit!'

We crowd around him.

'2000MM. 2048 code for storerooms. Ain't cooperating.'

Big Ben pauses before he speaks. 'They might've changed it to 2100.'

'Maybe. Only the double M's fixed.' He taps the box. 'No go. Leaps, THINK. What would Le Temps go for? When was he born?'

'2008.' Big Ben and I answer at the same time. Le Temps who is Pete LMS was born the same year as us.

It doesn't work.

GMT scrunches up her face. 'Could be '68, '72. Might not even be a leap, guys. Le Temps is an Annual. He could choose anything.'

'Millennia said I'd destroyed a CENTURY of work.'

MC² wriggles his body. He wants to disappear, appear, but can't. 'She founded the centre 2000, it's now 2100. 2100 don't work.'

He holds his hands up to the sky like he's trying to catch rain. GMT's raising her eyebrows like she's asking me a question. I take a deep breath like I'm going to run the 100 metres.

'What if it's 1900?'

No one moves. I tap the digits into the box followed by MM. Nothing happens. Then we hear a creaking noise and the floor starts moving under our feet like a lift. A hidden shaft!

'Maestro, Elle!' says MC^2 as we slowly descend to Minus 2 and the voices increase in volume until they turn into teens. The missing Leaplings!

∞

It takes a little while to see properly; it's so much darker down here. The walls are brown and the lighting isn't so bright. There are lots of machines that make it look like a factory. It must be where they do the meat-packing. The Leaplings look like normal teenagers except they stare at us without blinking and are wearing brown jumpsuits the colour of sacks and are standing behind the machines. But the machines haven't been turned on. No one says anything. They stopped talking as soon as we landed. Then a very short boy with black electric-shock hair steps forward.

'I'm Jack. Have you come to give us food? Have you come to give us food?'

'Far out,' says GMT. 'He's looping speech. You only do that when you get stuck in a year too long. How long you guys been down here?'

The Leaplings say nothing. They don't know. How do you count the days when you're looping with no watch?

There are SEVEN missing Leaplings: Jack, who must be 4-leap even though he's tiny, who was kidnapped from Leap

2044, the same trip Kwesi was on; three friends who came from 2032 called Yola, Lola and Shola who did illegal leaps from their day school; and three other Leap teens who were born in leap years they hated so couldn't wait to escape but got rounded up and forced to work here. They squint at us like people who've just got out of bed, and even when they turn their heads they do it in slow motion like robots. Le Temps must have threatened to shoot them with his Chronophone if they didn't work in his factory. I want to ask them lots of questions, like why didn't they leap to escape, but what actually comes out of my mouth is:

'Did Le Temps steal your DNA so you can't leap any more?'

'I don't understand.' Jack is the only one who will talk to us. 'We tried to leap on our own and holding hands but we got ill ill. They made us run round and round and round and round and round the field then go in the lab and spit in bowls. Then injected us for our blood. Then they gave us any food we wanted. I had chocolate cake. Are you robots?'

'No, we're Leaplings.'

Lola steps forwards, twiddling her long brown plait. 'They were nice to us at first. They let us play computer games. Said they'd contact our parents to say we were OK when our phones didn't work. Said it was like being on holiday.'

'But they lied.' Jack again. 'We started getting headaches from the games. I think they were designed to make us to make us confused. Then they brought us down here to work the machines. There were no clocks and our phones didn't work so we didn't know what the time was. We only stopped when the robots brought us food. Have you come to give us food?'

GMT shakes her head slowly. 'Le Temps wanted their DNA and their silence. He couldn't let them escape to tell the world. He used them to do what robots do. Run the machines.'

We look around the factory, then back at the Leaplings. They don't know what to do with the machines switched off. Some of them seem to have forgotten how to speak. I don't think stealing your DNA would take away your voice but I have lots of questions that come out in a string before I can stop them.

'Did all of you try to leap solo? When you got ill, did you vomit? Have you seen the sheap?'

MC^2 coughs. 'Forget Genetic Switch; Glitch is the problem. Le Temps deliberately chose 2100 so leaps would stay put. It's not a leap year, remember. Much much harder to leap unless you got The Gift in spades. Impossible to leap if your brain's mixed. You seen Kwesi?'

They all shake their heads.

'We have to find Noon,' I say.

'I'm hungry,' says Jack. 'Have you come to give us food?'

I think about going to the woods to pick mushrooms. Season taught me which ones are OK to eat and which ones will kill you. Big Ben rummages in his bag and takes out a bread roll. I squint my eyes at it. It can't possibly be. It IS.

'Don't eat it!' I shout and everyone looks at me. 'It's evidence.'

MC^2 smiles. 'Elle. Tell Leaps about the sheap.'

∞

Some of us want to leap and some of us want to seek. The seekers win.

'No one's going nowhere till we find Kwesi.'

I second that. Imagine if we got back to 2048 without Kwesi? Ama would never speak to us again. GMT stays in The Beanstalk with the Leaplings who are still eating like they haven't eaten for days and they haven't, not since the robots abandoned the centre and all the machinery stopped and they thought they'd die of starvation.

MC^2, Big Ben and I are walking up the spiral staircase to the first floor when we hear the music.

It's faint at first, like you're imagining it in your head, but as we continue up the stairs it gets louder, till we're taking two steps at a time like athletics training. I've heard music like this before, at the leap day celebration: that 1924 music Noon likes and she and Ama went crazy in their dancing, all arms and legs. Noon! We stop outside a door at the top of the stairs. Or rather, I stop, but MC^2 tries to open it, which is impossible because it doesn't have a handle.

'There's a code lock,' I say, and he taps in 1900MM. A second later, the door clicks open and the music stops.

'Careful,' I say. 'It could be a trap.'

We push the door in slow motion. The first thing we see is a large black wall covered in numbers and letters sprayed on like graffiti. But they're not flat against the wall. It's like the wall has come to life and is breathing. I squint my eyes and make out some of the symbols. $E=MC^2$, 2100 rotated all different angles, upside down, inside out, back to front. In the left-hand bottom corner, an unmistakable L with an infinity sign weaving in and out of it like a snake. Next to it, the thick black outline of a boy. Inside the outline, a tall black boy with round glasses, big ginger hair, white-and-black clothes like MC^2 and an infinity tattoo on his left hand.

I stare at the painting of the boy until it blinks! Slowly the painting that is a boy comes out of the wall towards us. Big Ben takes a step back. MC^2 swears under his breath and holds up his left fist like he's giving the Black Power salute in Mexico City in 1968. His voice sounds odd when he speaks, like he has a sore throat.

'The Squared missed a beat when you went phone-dead.'

The boy looks at him like he's looking twice, first through his eyes, then through his glasses. Very slowly, he holds up his left fist. They touch fists, clap palms, snap fingers till it sounds like a rap. Then they make all kinds of shapes with their hands like they're sculpting air. A sign dance. MC^2 turns to face us.

'Elle. Big Ben. KWESI. Kwesi. ELLE. BIG BEN.'

Kwesi holds up his fist to greet us. I do the same but Big Ben doesn't move forwards. I hope he's not going to hit Kwesi. He only just met him.

'Why are you here and not in the Minus 2?'

Kwesi makes rapid movements with his hands and face. MC^2 raises his eyebrows.

'Kwesi says he worked for Le Temps undercover in black

gloves to hide the tat. But Le Temps got wise. Put him in solitary.' He waits till Kwesi drops his hands. 'To try to make him switch sides, brother got special treatment. Beats. Paints.'

Big Ben pauses a long time before he speaks. 'Logical.'

Kwesi raises his fist to Big Ben and points to the red hat. Big Ben takes off the hat and hands it to Kwesi. I can't imagine how it's going to fit on his head over the afro. Big Ben tries to smooth down his hair but it still looks scruffy. In slow motion, he raises his left fist to meet Kwesi's.

'We still haven't found Noon,' I say.

Kwesi jerks his head towards me on the word Noon and draws a big circle with his hand then claps his hands fast twice. We don't need a translation. We should have thought of it before. Noon loved The Round. If she was going to leap anywhere in 2100, that's where she'd go.

∞

Noon doesn't look dazed like the other Leaplings. I guess she's not been here as long. Luckily she didn't leap to January 2100 by mistake.

'Le Temps told me to work for him. I said no. I leapt in The Round to escape. Kwesi said 2100. I KNEW you'd be here.' Noon smiles at Kwesi from East to West. I've never seen her look so happy.

'You did good,' says MC^2.

'There's 13 of us now,' I say. 'A group leap might work.'

Kwesi shakes his head and holds up various fingers like he's playing the piano. MC^2 explains.

'Brother don't like 13. Says 12 is best. He'll stay behind.'

I stare at him with an open mouth. 'What about Ama? She'll be furious if you don't go back. She'll roll her eyes anticlockwise. She can't leap to 2100.'

Kwesi looks at me as if he can see right into my head. Then he signs to me. I don't understand what he's signing but I like how he moves his hands and fingers. You can almost imagine the sound.

'Kwesi says: you speak sense. Big Ben should leap by car. And the sheap must be centre of the leap.'

∞

12 of us form a Chrono in The Round. In the middle is the prize sheap we called Ewe because she's female. We're going to transport her like luggage. We'll drop off Leaplings to their destination years and take Ewe back to 2048 to give to Season as a pet so she can use the poo to grow vegetables. We close our eyes and concentrate on the first stop, the 29th of February 2044. Jack wants to go back to the day he went missing. It's smooth this time, nothing like the 6-chrono-leap from 2020 or the 3-chrono-leap here. 12 is definitely best.

Yet before I open my eyes I know something isn't right. Before MC^2 consults his Chronophone and Kwesi signs something about the number 12 and Jack starts sniffing like he has a cold.

The leap hasn't worked. We're stuck in 2100.

I hate 2100. It's like the end of the world because no one lives here except the robots and even the robots have gone. Le Temps chose a good year to hide his crimes. We look at each other in the Chrono. How will we ever get back to Leap 2048?

'Can anyone know the time without a phone?'

Thankfully, Big Ben hasn't leapt in Fiona yet. He's good at problem solving so might come up with a plan. I concentrate.

'Le Temps said you have to look at the stars but he's a REAL criminal so it's a lie.'

'Today's the 28th of February?'

'The same, bro. You got a theory?'

'2100's not a leap year. The maths can't fit. But midnight today . . .'

We listen to Big Ben's theory about leap days and leap seconds. Leap seconds are usually added to the end of a year if things have got out of synch. But as this is an out-of-synch that should have been a leap year, anything could happen.

'If you leap the nanosecond after midnight tonight, leap power gets stronger.'

'You think we should leap then?' I say.

'Impossible is nothing,' says GMT.

MC^2 is nodding his head. 'The glitch might unstitch in the pitch.'

We sit in the dark for what seems like hours, find the Big

Dipper and the North Star because even though Le Temps is a real criminal he DOES know about time and the weather. Big Ben works it out mathematically. We hold hands again just before midnight, say goodbye to Big Ben and this time it works.

The journey back in time begins.

Chapter 22:00

INFINITES

MC^2, GMT, Kwesi, Noon and I leap back to The Round, 2048, just in time for breakfast because we're starving, tether Ewe to a tree and walk down to The Beanstalk. Big Ben does a good job in Fiona this time. I think Fiona helped with the supercharge. She doesn't look any more squeezed than she did in 2100. He's parked her where she usually is. Seconds later, Season's outside. She doesn't look at any of us, goes straight to Fiona, inspecting all the dents and taking photos of them on her Chronophone.

It's strange seeing the centre filled with people again, everyone at breakfast sitting in their rows, munching on red muffins, white rolls, yellow bananas. Ama's sitting with Eve near the food counters. She looks up when we walk in, gasps and runs over faster than leaping.

'Kwesi!'

Ama cries. She's crying because she's happy and sad at the

same time but I think she'll be OK because she hasn't seen Kwesi for years and now he's here.

Millennia comes over to us. I'm scared she might kill me in front of everybody because I destroyed a CENTURY of work. She looks like she's having a fight with her face. Her wrinkles are deeper than when we arrived a few days ago.

'Welcome back, Time Travellers. Please eat. You are just in time for an early graduation.'

Big Ben immediately goes to the counter and loads up his plate. That boy eats from morning to night. No wonder he's growing faster than bamboo. I'm glad he's gone to get food because Season just came back into The Beanstalk. She doesn't say a word. Just looks at us, which is worse because we don't know whether she's Power Surging or doing Anger Management. Her face is red and scrunched up like a fist. I wish she would say something because if she doesn't she might hit Big Ben and it'll be Armageddon.

∞

Graduation is horrid. Everyone's upset because we've only been here half a week. We're supposed to graduate on Saturday morning and it's only Wednesday. Big Ben and Season are late because he was giving her Ewe as a present to make her face go back to normal. As Season takes her chair on stage, next to MC^2, Millennia humiliates Big Ben in front of the whole hall.

'Is the most famous clock in the world, Big Ben, as bad as you at keeping time?'

When people go up to the stage to get their Leap Permits, they refuse to shake hands with Millennia. At the very end of the ceremony, she clears her throat like grown-ups do when they're going to say something important.

'Due to the unfortunate circumstances surrounding our trusted colleague, Mr T, Leap 2048 will terminate after lunch today.'

Martin Aston swears and Maria says her mum's going to ask for a total refund, which is better than swearing in Portuguese. But I don't get upset because I know that we just had graduation and after graduation you have to go home. We're told to pack our clothes and vacate the centre by 2 p.m. Millennia waits until it's quiet before she speaks again.

'I founded this centre in the 2000 millennium when I CREATED the Time Squad. Our objective: to FIGHT CRIME ACROSS TIME. We have been fighting crime for 48 years. During that time, much has been achieved that I am proud of. But,' she gives me the cat's-eye for three long seconds and I look away, 'the time has come for me to retire, to make way for other visions. I will NOT be idle.'

MC^2 and Season raise their eyebrows so high they get lost in their hair. Millennia didn't tell them. Does that mean they have to run the centre themselves until they get a new boss? Or is the Time Squad totally finished? What's Millennia going to do, now she's not managing the centre? Is she going to spend a whole century taking revenge?

∞

GMT, Big Ben and I are speaking in whispers in case someone's outside the Common Room listening. GMT wanted to talk to us, alone. I'm tired now. Everything's happened so fast. Again, I'm confused. If it's 2048, has this really happened yet or is it still going to happen? She's saying something about Millennia being upset because Le Temps was her favourite colleague who helped her develop the centre; then something about the Predictive and I pay more attention. That it might have been sent by an infinite number of possible other individuals with an infinite number of reasons. SOS L could have an infinite number of interpretations. I can see Big Ben likes this because he starts listing all the possibilities till I'm scared he'll go on forever.

But I like GMT talking about infinity because it's my favourite mathematical symbol, a figure 8 lying on its side: ∞. Something without a beginning or end. I used to doodle the sign in primary school until I got into trouble because I wouldn't stop. Real infinity's scary, though. I like to know when things start and stop. But I'm getting better at coping with things I can't see.

GMT's obsessed with time. She may not look at her watch 24 hours a day any more, but she keeps on about what you do in the present changing the future.

'That text, Elle. If you rewrite the future, it can mean different things. Might not even happen at all. Save Pete LMS, save the planet!'

'What do you mean?'

'Be his buddy.'

'He's a bully!'

'Who's gonna be punished. OK, you don't have to befriend him, you got friends already. He likes you. Maybe if you were nice to him, he might . . .' She shrugs her shoulders. 'You might be able to prevent all this.'

'He's not God. He didn't invent global warming.'

'Maybe not. But one small act could change the world. Ever heard of the Butterfly Effect?'

Big Ben knows the answer. We all wait to hear what he has to say. But at that moment MC^2 appears out of nowhere.

'Leaps,' he blinks, 'what happened in the hall, forget it. You ain't graduated yet. You and Big Ben just got promoted.'

'To the Time Squad?' I say. How can we help run the Time Squad when we're only 3-leap? That's too young, even in the future.

'No. The Infinites. Time Squad's past tense. You freeze-framed Le Temps. We need your skills.'

'I can't because I'm only 3-leap and I'm not allowed to have a tattoo until I'm 4-leap and I can't live in the future because Grandma wouldn't have anyone to make her pepper soup when her leg is paining her.'

'No probs, sis. You got the symbol anyways. Carved two more in The Round. Symbolising you and Big Ben. You get the tat when you level up.'

I open my mouth to a capital O. That explains the two extra ∞ signs on the trees. He predicted we'd become Infinites before the Predictive! He's still talking.

'You got no choice. Millennia's speech . . .' He shakes his

head. 'You faced the Predictive. Now you gotta face down Millennia.' He pauses. 'An' your man leapt 52 years in a race car.' He disappears, appears on the same spot. 'You don't have to LIVE here, just leap, Leaps.

'Infinites need numbers. We gotta stop the eco-crimes. ROOT FOR THE FUTURE. When Leaps kept vanishing an' I came to your school, I was head-hunting.'

'Is our headteacher a criminal too?'

'No, sis. Head-hunting's recruitment. I needed kids who took no spit, Leaps scorin' high on the PPF.' He looks at me and Big Ben. 'You two just passed initiation.'

Big Ben scrunches up his forehead. 'Is it like a ROAD for the future?'

'I meant R O O T, but ya know what? It could be R O U T E as well. Maestro, Ben!' He looks at his watch. 'Meet you at The Round. In five.'

∞

Kwesi, Noon, Ama and Eve are already there. You need eight people for the ceremony, to make the infinity sign. Kwesi looks at no one in particular, making shapes with his hands.

'Kwesi says choose a letter or the letter will choose you,' says MC^2. 'He means an initial, like the Time Squad. I'm E, GMT is G, Kwesi's K. It's better you choose one yourself. Gives it more grav.'

I look at Big Ben. He's obviously going to go for B. But I can't be E for Elle. That letter's already taken. Then I have an idea.

'Could I be L?' I say. 'Cos it's a homophone of Elle?'

MC² looks pleased. 'Maestro! And it'll remind Leaps you brought down Le Temps with SOS L. You'll go down in PPF.'

'And I'm B for Ben,' says Big Ben, and MC² gives him a high-five.

Then the eight of us hold hands to form the infinity sign, in silence, according to tradition. I'm desperate to ask lots of questions but know it will spoil the ceremony and Ama will roll her eyes anticlockwise and we'll have to start all over again. I'm glad Ama's at the ceremony, though, because she likes Leaplings when she's not angry with us. She's an honorary Leapling, like Bob Beamon.

After the ceremony, Kwesi draws an imaginary infinity sign on our left hands, over and over, till it feels like it will never go away. GMT smiles.

'You and Big Ben are Level 1 Infinites. You passed the first test. Initiation.'

Big Ben says, 'Are there infinite tests?'

and I say, 'What's the second test?'

at exactly the same time.

'There's four in all: Initiate, Intermediate and Infinite. Me, Kwesi and MC are Infinites. You don't know what it is till it happens.'

'That's only three,' says Big Ben.

GMT looks at Kwesi, Kwesi looks at MC², MC² looks at GMT like they're passing the baton in a permanent relay.

'Only one person's ever passed the fourth. And lived,' she says.

'Who's that?' I say, but I think I know.

'Infinity.'

That name again. Who is it? Who is it?

'Where's Infinity?'

'Anywhere and everywhere,' says MC^2, popping up all over the place so quickly I think there's ten of him. GMT gives him the bull's-eye and he stops.

'We ain't met her. She just kinda gives orders. We obey.'

Kwesi and GMT nod their heads. I do what-big-eyes. How can you take orders from someone you never met? And how do they know Infinity's a woman if they never met her? I meant to ask him WHO'S Infinity but I think he answered my question.

I look around at my circle of friends. This is the happiest I've ever been in three leap years. At 2 p.m. I won't say goodbye. I'll say *au revoir*, which means until I see you again. I know the criminal Le Temps said it to Millennia, but I'll say it for a good reason. I might not see Ama as easily, though, because she's an Annual. She can't leap back to 2020 to see me. This makes me sad.

'I don't want to go home. I may never see you again.'

'Don't count on that, sis,' she says, giving me her gap-toothed grin. 'I can't leap but you can. Track me down through MC^2 or Kwesi.'

I think about Annuals not being able to leap. 'Will Le Temps get ad infinitum?' I say.

Kwesi looks at me and signs: 'The sentence will equal the crime.' He pauses until everyone is looking at him, then moves his hands like he's conducting an orchestra. MC^2 translates.

'Not ad infinitum cos he didn't kill no one. But he'll be locked up at least a decade. Course, if he reforms in 2020, he might not turn criminal in '48. The future needs the past to become itself.'

'Kwesi's right,' says GMT. 'Only you and Big Ben can reverse this. Save Pete LMS, no missing Leaps, no stolen DNA, no sheap!'

'I can't be nice to Pete LMS,' I say. 'He's a monster. Anyway, Big Ben will fight him!'

'No, I won't,' says Big Ben immediately.

'I could stop calling him Pete LMS, I suppose.'

I think it through. If he's not called Pete LMS, he can't become Le Temps because he can't make the anagram and think he's so special. If he doesn't become Le Temps, he won't be able to buy the land for the centre and put Leapling DNA into sheep and sell sheap to those who can afford it.

'What WILL you call him?' says Big Ben. 'And will you call me B from now on?'

'No,' I say. 'I'll call you Ben. Or Big Ben. BB for short, I guess.'

'Elle.' There's a long pause. His face is bright pink and his voice sounds deeper than usual, like a man's. 'Sorry I said boys are stronger than girls. I'm scared you'd be sick in 2100. I didn't like you to leap on your own.'

'That's OK. I forgive you!'

'Am I your boyfriend?'

'No. You're my boy friend. My best friend.'

I hold out my hand and he takes it. I squeeze it and smile.

Big Ben smiles back.

Chapter 23:00

3-LEAP

Grandma's waiting outside the front door when Mrs C Eckler drops me off at 10:30 a.m. There are two bags of shopping at her feet, bulging with food. While I was away, she managed to go shopping on her own! She looks like she's aged 20 years; she can hardly lift her hand to put the key in the door.

'Elle Bíbi-Imbelé. Welcome back! God has given you safe journey.'

She hugs me very tight and sings her welcome song. I'm happy to see Grandma again and glad she didn't stay at the bottom of the stairs for hours.

I have to take the bags upstairs in two trips because they're so heavy. Flour, sugar, eggs in one bag. Yams, beans flour, chicken and fish in the other. It's strange to see chicken again, having spent all week eating vegan food. I didn't eat anything Le Temps cooked. But Le Temps seems a long way away and a long time ago, even though he's in the future. Grandma sometimes buys chicken for Sunday dinner or if we have guests.

'Na special occasion. You have come of age.'

When Grandma cooks, she cooks for the whole village, even though she left Nigeria years ago, rarely goes back and we don't socialise with the other tenants. Who does she think will eat all this food? No one in church knows it's my birthday. Maybe she'll invite them round tomorrow after the service. She's always pretended my birthday's on the 1st of March. But I hope she doesn't invite them. There'll be too many people speaking at the same time and I'll get a headache. But it's nice Grandma's acknowledging I've come of age at 3-leap, that 12 is an important age for Leaplings, like 13 is for Annuals.

We're going to cook chicken, fried fish, moi-moi, jellof rice and fried yam. We would have made pepper soup but Grandma already made some so I had something to eat as soon as I got back. I feel funny about eating the fish, so don't put any in my bowl. I have three chunks of yam, though. I've missed having yam every day. I wonder what happened to the rest of the yams in 2048. Maybe Season made soup with them.

We're also going to make birthday cake. It will be cake with eggs, not the vegan cake Season made, but I won't refuse it or Grandma will be sad. She walked all the way to the shops to buy food and carried it all the way home, though her legs were paining her.

Grandma lays all the food out on the table. She'll make the cake because it's my birthday and the cake is her gift. I'll help her with the savouries. She gives me instructions. But I know how to cook and she knows I know. She just likes to talk. Maybe she missed me those few hours I was away from 2020. She doesn't seem surprised I came home early. If Leap 2048 had gone to plan and Le Temps hadn't tried to kill me and got arrested, I would have got home after 3 p.m. But Mrs C Eckler decided because the trip was unexpectedly cut short we all deserved more time at home to celebrate 3-leap with our families.

I hear knocking on the downstairs door but ignore it. We're not expecting anyone and my fingers are covered with onion juice. I've chopped the onions fine fine so they break down more easily in the blender with some water. Grandma even got some white tomatoes so the stew will remain white. I've never seen white tomatoes before. She must have ordered them specially. That was a kind thing to do. We can use the same stew for the jellof rice and moi-moi.

Someone's knocking again, more persistently this time, like it's the postman and he's got a parcel that's too big to fit through the letterbox. Grandma looks at me.

'Elle, answer the door!'

I'm cross because I have to wash my hands and I haven't finished chopping the onions but I do what Grandma says. I never disobey her. I trudge down the stairs and have to sort out all the latches before I open the door because we had a break-in a month ago and the thieves stole some stuff from downstairs. They never stole anything from our flat. We don't own anything they would want to steal.

It's Big Ben!

'You didn't text,' I say.

Big Ben's only visited our flat twice and both times he texted before he arrived. He shrugs his shoulders.

'Left my phone at home. Haven't been home yet.'

Big Ben follows me up the stairs. Our flat door is already open.

'You are welcome!'

Grandma gives Big Ben a big hug and a huge bowl of pepper soup. He eats it in two minutes without coughing and asks for more. Maybe he's a Nigerian in disguise.

'Make tea for this your boyfriend!'

'Grandma, he's not my boyfriend.'

Grandma smiles as if she hasn't heard me and continues to blend the onions, singing as she does. It's a bit noisy but we can cope with the noise. I can hear knocking on the door, AGAIN. I can't remember the last time it was so busy. I check my phone for the time and realise there's several texts, all from 2048.

AMA SENDS HER LOVE

SEASON AND EWE SAY HELLO

CAN WE VISIT?

HAVE CHRONOPHONE FOR YOU!

More knocking. I don't think Big Ben heard it, he's so busy slurping his soup, devouring the huge chunks of white fish. I go downstairs to answer it. MC^2 and GMT! It feels odd seeing them here, outside my flat, in 2020. Wrong. Like an Anachronism. I stare at them, not sure what to do. They belong in 2048.

'Party time!' says GMT. She's wearing a full-length turquoise velvet dress with mermaids embroidered on the sleeves. MC^2 has a bag slung over his shoulder that looks exactly like Big Ben's but much newer.

'Don't worry, sis,' he says. 'Special delivery for specialist Leaps. Chronophones. So you stay connected.' He lowers his voice. 'Elle, we need to come inside. Keep stuff private.'

I understand. Chronophones haven't been invented yet so we don't want people to see them. Especially outside my flat. The thieves would come and steal them and commit even more crimes than Le Temps. I let them in.

I've never seen Grandma look so happy, like she knew they'd come, sitting them down at the table, making me introduce everybody, make them tea and eat pepper soup whether they like it or not. Even GMT sips the soup. No one can refuse Grandma. She moves across the room without limping and I wonder if her leg doesn't pain so much when she's happy. Or maybe she doesn't notice the pain with lots of people to talk to.

She tells me to talk to my friends while she continues to prepare the food. I like that she calls them my friends. I haven't had friends in 2020 before and never had them in the flat. Only Big Ben. I don't even worry I didn't have time to scrub the mushrooms off the walls. No one's noticed the mushrooms. I don't know what to say to them, though, so I say:

'Where are the Chronophones?'

MC^2 puts two silver Chronophones on the table. They're identical, except one has a B and the other an L inscribed underneath. Big Ben picks his up and starts clicking. 30 seconds later he's whooping and punching the air. I check his phone. A video of Fiona soaring over the countryside, Season at the wheel, playing on a loop. It'll take him an hour to calm down. Then I'll remind him to text his mum so she knows he's safe. At least she's not expecting him home till after 3 p.m. I pick up my Chronophone.

'Customised, too,' says MC^2. 'Check out the vid. Ama's maestro leap.'

I click on the video icon and the words 'AMA'S LEAP OF THE CENTURY' come onto the screen in white letters, like she's famous. Then the camera shows Ama at the end of the run-up of the long jump. She's talking to herself like athletes do so the words become a reality. Then she stretches back, pauses, and begins to accelerate down the runway. I've never seen Ama run like this before. She's quite fast. Then she hits the board and hurls herself into the air. Then everything goes slow motion until she lands, twisting her body to the side so she doesn't fall back. It must be at least 6 metres! The words '6 metres 2 centimetres' come onto the screen then fizzle out to Ama's talking head. She says:

'Elle, wish I could leap like you, but I do my best. Stay in touch, sis!!'

I look back up at MC^2. I don't know whether to be happy because Ama has made me a brilliant video or sad because she can't come to my birthday. And I thought she didn't like athletics. MC^2 smiles.

'Almost as good as your man, Bob Beamon.'

I smile back as the Bob Beamon video replays in my head. The run-up, the jump, the commentary. I've barely thought about Bob Beamon for two days. The last two days of Leap 2048 were so full of Oopses. But I almost never thought of Bob Beamon. Maybe I've changed.

Grandma turns from the sideboard, where she's just added the last flour to the cake mixture. I can see it's a real effort for her to mix but I don't offer to help. She wants to make the cake on her own.

'Elle, did I not teach you manners in this England?'

She's reminding me to say thank you for the present. In Nigeria, some people don't say please or thank you at all. They think it's very English to do that. But some Nigerians say please and thank you all the time. That's how they learnt English. Grandma's like that.

∞

Everyone stays for the birthday tea. Grandma puts on the special white tablecloth, the one we use for guests, extends the table and lays the food out in the middle. It's a real feast. I tell GMT she can eat the moi-moi and rice because we never use meat stock in it. And the fried yam. Grandma's looking at GMT with her what-big-eyes. She takes a deep breath like she's going to run the 100 metres, though she can barely walk it. I wonder what she's going to say.

'This your boyfriend enjoys his food-o! A man likes his meat. But you,' looking at GMT, 'you are vegetarian?'

'Yes, ma'am,' says GMT.

Grandma smiles. 'I am very pleased with you. Some members of our church do not let meat pass their lips. They say man and beast have all one breath. Man should not have pre-eminence above a beast.'

Everyone goes quiet. I'm thinking about MAN=BEAST, Le Temps mixing Leapling DNA with sheep DNA to make sheap to kill and sell to those who can afford it. I'm glad Grandma isn't anti-vegetarianism. Maybe she won't mind so much that I'm a flexitarian now. I've decided to only eat meat on special occasions. Like this. Or if someone's cooked it and I don't want to be rude. Mrs C Eckler says I shouldn't give up meat and fish completely until I'm able to eat food in colours other than white, so I get a balanced diet.

I can't say the same for Big Ben. He eats so much of everything, I worry he's going to be sick. But he's never sick. And I think Grandma wants to adopt him as her honorary grandson. Then she can feed him pepper soup every morning for breakfast.

Before we eat, Grandma blesses the food and our safe passage from Leap 2048, that our enemies did quake and perish and our table be plentiful on this our special day.

Grandma must know about Le Temps and Millennia. But how? And I like she said 'our enemies', even though she wasn't there. She was shopping for this party. I want to ask so many questions but I'm learning when to speak and when not to speak. I can ask her another time. Not now. Not today.

Today is a special day. Today is the 29th of February 2020. It's my 3rd leap birthday. I'm officially allowed to leap on my own. And I'm now a Level 1 Infinite. I can help save the planet. All my friends are Leaplings except Ama, who's an Annual. Grandma's not a Leapling but she's my family. The food tastes nice. Maybe one day we'll all be Vegans. Maybe one day there'll be no more fish in the sea. Or maybe human beings will fall in love with Planet Earth. The future needs the past to become itself.

Grandma rises from the table and I help her clear the food away. We wipe the surface with a fresh cloth. Then she puts three candles on the cake and lights them with a match. It's a plain cake, with no filling, no icing, only one layer. But it's still warm from the oven and the smell makes me happy. It's the most special cake in the world. Grandma lifts the cake, opens her mouth and begins to sing 'Happy Birthday'. Everyone joins in. When we get to the name, we don't know what to sing. It's not just my 3rd leap birthday today, it's Big Ben's too. Most people sing 'Elle' but I sing 'Big Ben'. MC^2 and GMT are 4-leap. That means they're grown-ups. Today, every true Leapling is celebrating, even if they pretend they were born on the 28th of February or the 1st of March.

'Happy birthday to you,' we all sing.

The song's over. Grandma places the cake in the middle of the table. I stare into the three flames, take a deep breath like I'm going to push out of the blocks for the 100 metres.

And blow them out.

∞ Chapter 00:00 ∞

CONTINUUM

It isn't easy being nice to Pete LMS.

We've been back in school a month. Big Ben doesn't like me being nice to another boy but has promised not to hit him so hard he dives into the air like the Fosbury Flop. Every time I see Pete LMS, I remember him humiliating me in front of the whole class. But he doesn't bully me now. He WAS excluded for a week after the SOS L episode and he DID say sorry. I've stopped calling him Pete LMS behind his back. I have to take a deep breath after I say Pete, to stop myself saying LMS. When I'm nice to him, like picking up his pencil when it drops on the floor in double maths, he raises his eyebrows so high, his forehead wrinkles like he's turned into Le Temps and I'm scared. But I'm a Level 1 Infinite and supposed to be brave. No one knows I'm a Level 1 Infinite except everyone at the ceremony and you. It has to be secret so we can stop eco-crimes. You mustn't tell anyone.

Today, Big Ben's at Anger Management in Action, where

you're allowed to shout and break real chairs under supervision. I notice Pete looking at me in double English, and when I look at him he looks away. Why's he constantly staring at me? MC^2 sends a text:

THE FUTURE JUST GOT BETTER

Does the future only get better if the present gets worse? I get a headache imagining the future happening at the same time as the present.

Now, it's lunchtime. I'm sitting on the bench by the track eating grilled halloumi in white flatbread when Pete comes over and clears his throat.

'How fast can you run the 100 metres?' he says.

I do what-big-eyes. '13.12 seconds, which gives me an 87.64% age grade, now I'm 12.'

I turn away from him but he doesn't go away.

'Elle.' He pauses a long time. 'I know you and Big Ben . . . but, I wondered if . . .'

I turn to face him. 'What?'

'Would you go running with me?'

'No. I won't two-time Big Ben!'

His face goes bright red and his voice goes a bit squeaky. 'Thought so. He's A List. I'm a non-scorer.'

He means in competitions. As are the fastest, Bs slower but still score, non-scorers can take part but don't get points for the team. It must be hard if you're good but two people are always better than you. I feel sad when I think that.

'I could teach you the long jump.'

Pete stares at me like I just disappeared and appeared on the spot. I'm surprised myself. It was my mouth speaking before my brain had time to stop it.

'OK,' he says and walks away.

The back of his ears are still red. I'm a bit worried Big Ben will be jealous but he's not interested in long jump, only track and cross country. And he knows we have to be nice to Pete. My Chronophone buzzes in my bag. I know, without looking, it isn't Big Ben telling me how many chairs he's broken. It's MC^2.

The future just got even better.

∞

I'm starting to like the future even more than the past. You can't predict how it's going to happen, it changes so much. You have to do good things in the present to help the future. One thing I know: I'm definitely a Level 1 Infinite, though I became one in the future. I proved myself and I passed the test. It can't unhappen. Some things from the future ARE fixed. When I go there again, it won't be to fight Le Temps. Le Temps doesn't exist in the future any more, now Pete LMS is Pete.

Millennia doesn't hate me in this changed future because she can't employ a non-existent Le Temps to build her business for me to destroy. Millennia hates me RIGHT NOW for something that has already happened in HER past, MY future. Sometime in the future I'll leap back to the past and thwart Millennia.

Maybe that will be my next test. If I pass, I'll become an Intermediate. I've been in training to improve my leap skills. Everyone at athletics club thinks it's to improve my accuracy on the board for the long jump but I'm doing it undercover. I'm really training so the next time I leap, I leap to a nanosecond. I haven't even told Big Ben but I think he'll like it.

Acknowledgements

I would not have written *The Infinite* without my two wonderful sons, Solomon and Valentine, encouraging me to read the books they'd fallen in love with. Boys, you took me away from gritty adult realism to alternative realities, at times equally gritty, at times fantastical. Solomon, you reminded me young readers like action, action, action; Valentine, you invented the Ferrari Forever and PPF and gave me perceptive, enthusiastic feedback for the very first draft. When you announced, several summers ago, you were both going to write novels, I thought, if you can do it, so can I.

And here it is!

There are other young people I'd like to thank who read early versions of the book: my niece, Esther, for that upbeat email where you said you'd recommend it to your classmates; Eleanor for persevering even though reading's not your thing; Oliver for loving the book and grilling me about the publishing process whilst simultaneously stewarding Junior Parkrun; and Grace for appreciating the characters of Elle, Ama and GMT. May you continue to thrive as a reader AND a writer!

There are numerous grown-ups who went out of their way to make *The Infinite* possible. If I mentioned you all, this book would be twice the size. I particularly want to thank my husband, Jeremy, who encouraged me to write a novel in the first place, gave not only positive feedback and brainstorming sessions but love and support. You enabled me to immerse myself in the imaginary world for months at a time and never once complained when I forgot to cook half the dinner. My father, Clement Agbabi, for believing in me as a writer since I was a very young child, and for giving me advice about the impossible task of transposing Izon into English. Mum and dad in Wales: mum, reading to me every night is the greatest gift you gave me. My immediate and extended family, in the UK and Nigeria for your belief in my abilities, especially cousin Jumbo, keep writing those stories. Faustie-Ann, I'm still waiting for that autobiography.

I'm so lucky to have friends who are also superb writers and readers. I thank Steve Tasane for his unbridled enthusiasm for the concept from the very beginning, the detailed, invaluable plotting suggestions for that early draft. Rosemary Harris for helping me create child-friendly peril, especially relating to genetic modification. I cannot thank you enough. Ros Barber for the Creative Writing PhD reference and enabling the light to get in. Kate Clanchy for recommending screenwriting books for plotting. Nina Tullar for sending a brilliant screenwriting book out of the blue. I LOVED storyboarding. Leone Ross, for the way you said the word 'novelist' with a twinkle in your eye. I felt ten feet tall. Bernardine Evaristo for supporting me as a writer on so many levels. Without you, I would not be where I am today. Courttia Newland for that excellent Spread the Word sci-fi workshop, complete with Star Wars-inspired video link. Stephanie Scott for sharing authorial advice and delicious meals in London when I most needed them. Kim Zarins for being so positive though you'd only just met me, your words of advice around middle-grade children's books. The Medieval and Renaissance Women's Drinking Society, for continuing to nurture and celebrate all our achievements, past, present and future.

I'd like to thank friends who are not writers who have helped me in incalculable ways. Stephen Logan for the PhD reference, then reminding me, when I chose not to go ahead with it, that I was capable of writing a novel without the academic framework. Emma, you encouraged your children to read that early draft and read it yourself, even though you're a very busy maths teacher! And for introducing me to both Parkruns. Rebecca, for our walks and talks. You've been rooting for Elle from the outset. Jo, you were so thrilled when I got the text from Canongate and I rushed out of your house to make that phone call. Stephen G, for your absolute joy when you heard I'd written a novel. Anne-Marie for recommending Black speculative fiction on the way back from the school run.

All this would be behind closed doors if I didn't have one of the most innovative and dynamic publishers ever. Thank you to the entire team at Canongate for their excitement about this book. I especially want to thank Jamie Byng, for publishing my poetry as early as 2000 and even then, encouraging me to write a novel. It's only taken me 20 years! Francis Bickmore, who responded to the concept in the early stages with such enthusiasm. You sent me that lovely email 45 pages in and continue to champion the book. Thank you so, so much. My editor, Jo Dingley, for always believing in Elle's voice, for your thoroughness and dedication to the micro and the macro of world-building, I'm forever indebted. Freelance copy editor, Debs Warner, for painstakingly editing all those double quote marks and numbers and still remaining positive about the text! Anna Frame for continuing to support me and my work with verve. Vicki Rutherford, Leila Cruickshank, Holly Domney and Megan Reid for coordinating the process and efficiently answering my endless queries. Leila, I'm in awe of your superhuman proofreading skills, spotting everything from the nitty-gritty of punctuation to the mammoth of a plot hole we all missed. The entire Art Team for creating a cover that made my boys say wow.

A very special thank you to Lizzie Huxley-Jones for your meticulous sensitivity read, reminding me that empathy is more important than euphony. You know Elle and her friends better than I know myself. I hope you enjoy the final edit.

Respect to my literary agent, Simon Trewin, for believing in the manuscript, for sharing it, for those rejuvenating meetings and witty one-liner emails. Thank you for enabling me to transition to this new literary form. My performance agents, Rochelle Saunders and Melanie Abrahams at Renaissance One, for staying with me despite my regular literary hibernations when I refused all sources of income. Your hard work and dedication are eternally appreciated.

To all the poets and promoters who invited me to read in the UK and abroad, especially the USA, enabling me to save up and take time out to write the first drafts; to all those who have been so positive when I declined subsequent poetry work, I hope you appreciate the wordplay.

Finally, I'd like to thank everyone at Dartford Harriers Athletic Club for giving me an alternative reality away from the computer that feeds back into the writing, especially Terry and Marion Povey for getting me back into sprinting after a 35-year gap; the entire Vets team; and Jill, Fleur, Allison and Christine, it's such a joy to train with you. Respect to Vets still brave enough to attempt the long jump!

© Lyndon Douglas Photography

Patience Agbabi was born in London in 1965 to Nigerian parents, spent her teenage years living in North Wales and now lives in Kent with her husband and children. She has been writing poetry for over twenty years; *The Infinite* is her first novel. Like Elle, she loves sprinting, numbers and pepper soup, but, disappointingly, her leaping is less spectacular.